MURDER AT THE PEKING OPERA

QING DYNASTY MYSTERIES BOOK 3

AMANDA ROBERTS

Murder at the Peking Opera

A Qing Dynasty Mystery

Murder at the Peking Opera

Amanda Roberts

Red Empress Publishing
www.RedEmpressPublishing.com

Cover by Cherith Vaughan
www.EmpressAuthorSolutions.com

ALSO BY AMANDA ROBERTS

Fiction

Threads of Silk

The Qing Dynasty Mysteries

Murder in the Forbidden City

Murder in the British Quarter

Murder at the Peking Opera

The Touching Time Series

The Emperor's Seal

The Empress's Dagger

The Slave's Necklace

Nonfiction

The Crazy Dumplings Cookbook

Crazy Dumplings II: Even Dumplinger

1

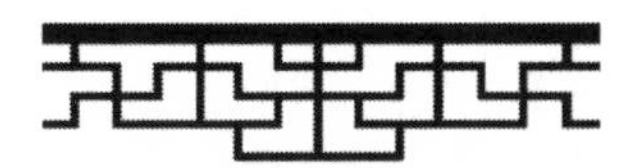

Lady Li cleared her throat and motioned for a maid to bring some more tea. She was doing her best to affect the air of superiority she usually carried, but the woman sitting across from her was a formidable opponent. She willed her foot to still, not tap, and to hold her teacup gingerly instead of gripping it like a vise.

"Of course, we are more than pleased our son has finally agreed to a marriage match," Gong Furen—Inspector Gong's mother—said as she held her head up and tried to look down her nose at Lady Li.

But no one looked down on Lady Li.

Lady Li had worn one of her most ornate chapaos, and her hair was perfectly styled around her batou headdress. The jewels she used to decorate her hair were large and gleamed even in the diluted light of the formal sitting room they were currently occupying in Lady Li's mansion.

Gong Furen had spared no effort in her own attire as well, but it was clear that her embroidery thread was not as expensive as Lady Li's and she owned far fewer jewels. But there were other areas where Gong Furen surpassed Lady

Li. Specifically in that she had sons, one of whom wanted to take Lady Li's companion and her late husband's former concubine, Swan, as his wife.

Gong Laoye, Inspector Gong's father, was present as well, but other than the prescribed greetings, he had remained silent. Allowing his wife to handle the negotiations. Lady Li suspected Gong Furen handled most aspects of their life together.

"But under the circumstances," Gong Furen continued, "you understand why we would...have concerns."

Lady Li smiled and gave a small nod. It was the "concerns" that threatened to show the cracks in her confidence. She wanted Inspector Gong's parents to accept the match, but in order to convince them, certain aspects of Concubine...*Lady* Swan's life would have to be...concealed. She did not want to deceive the Gongs, but Inspector Gong already knew about Swan's opium addiction and had agreed to marry her anyway. Revealing Swan's addiction to his parents would only make life for all of them much more difficult.

"I can assure you," Lady Li said, "that Lady Swan would be an excellent wife for your son."

Swan, appropriately, said nothing, but sat straight with her eyes downcast. Lady Li knew that Swan was eager for the marriage, but she really had no say in the matter. She was Lady Li's property, passed on to her after their husband's death. As such, it was at Lady Li's discretion what happened to the girl, whether she should marry or remain a chaste widow for the rest of her days. Similar to how Swan had had no choice in her first marriage either.

"I have no doubt of Lady Swan's many admirable qualities," Gong Furen acquiesced as she eyed the girl up and down. "I am sure your husband was a man of discerning taste."

"Indeed, he was," Lady Li said, motioning for the maid to refill their teacups. "Lady Swan is from a very respectable family here in Peking. Her father is a calligrapher. He taught his daughter to read and write, and he personally schooled her to have the most beautiful penmanship. She can recite all the classics and she speaks English."

"Yes," Gong Furen said, pressing her lips disapprovingly. "We heard how she...assisted our son on his last case. You know she turned up at our house, *unescorted*."

Lady Li felt her eye twitch and hoped it was not visible. Lady Li had been helping Inspector Gong solve a murder in the British Quarter of the Foreign Legation because she spoke English and he did not. Swan had taken it upon herself to sneak out of the mansion and involve herself in the case as well. She had been helpful, but Lady Li had feared the damage she could have done to her reputation. Married women—even widows—were rarely seen out of their homes, and never unescorted. But Swan had ended up going to Inspector Gong's home because she was—rightly—afraid of returning home to Lady Li, who would have beaten her soundly had Inspector Gong not been there to still her hand.

Lady Li gave a small chuckle, as if the incident had not been as serious as they all knew it was. "Lady Swan certainly showed her industriousness that day. I daresay Inspector Gong might not have been able to solve the case without her."

Gong Furen leaned back in her chair and sighed. "Yes, I do think that her usefulness to him on that occasion is why he has become so insistent on this match." She looked at her husband, Gong Laoye, but he stayed quiet, offering no help to his wife in this situation. It was clear that he would accept whatever ruling his wife made.

"I believe that Inspector Gong wants a wife who is both dutiful and useful," Lady Li offered. "One who will be able to raise his children and run his household while he is busy working for the prince and keeping the city safe."

"Gods willing, she won't have to run the household for many years," Gong Furen said. It was tradition for sons to stay with their family even after marriage. And Lady Li knew that Inspector Gong had older brothers who were already married as well. Even after Gong Furen passed away, Swan would be the least of the next generation of wives. Lady Li feared that Swan's desire to marry was blinding her to the difficulties of having to kowtow to a mother-in-law and elder sisters-in-law, but that was something that Swan would eventually learn on her own should the marriage happen.

"But raising children..." Gong Furen said, and Lady Li felt her heart clinch in her chest. "We do hope that sons would come quickly. Our son has waited much too long to accept a wife. We do not want to delay any children."

Lady Li nodded. "Of course," she said. "My husband passed away so soon after Swan joined our household, she was never blessed with a child of her own. But she has been a wonderful aunt to my daughters."

Please don't ask more. Please don't ask more, Lady Li prayed silently as Gong Furen looked at Swan again.

"Stand up, girl," Gong Furen ordered Swan. Swan glanced at Lady Li, who nodded her permission.

Swan stood up gracefully, not wobbling even for a moment on her pot-bottom shoes.

"Turn around," Gong Furen said, and Swan did so. Gong Furen tisked her tongue and shook her head. "She is awfully skinny. It could be difficult for her to bear healthy children."

Lady Li laughed again. "Nothing some heavy meals and happiness won't cure," Lady Li said, motioning for Swan to retake her seat. "She mourned greatly for Lord Yun when he passed. She fasted for months. Her normal appetite seems to have never returned to her. But I am sure that once she has a new husband to warm her heart and her bed, a robust appetite—and hearty sons—will follow."

"And she is already twenty years old?" Gong Furen asked, looking for every opportunity to undermine Swan's suitability as a wife.

Lady Li forced her disgust at the conversation down her throat. This was actually the first time Lady Li had been involved in marriage negotiations. She did not arrange her own marriage or Swan's, and her own daughters were not yet of a marrying age. She knew the general routine of the two families coming together to reach an agreement, but she didn't realize how offensive the whole process was, as though they were bartering over the quality and price of a new heifer.

"Yes," Lady Li finally said. "She was only sixteen when my husband took her as a concubine, and that was four years ago."

"A concubine," Gong Furen said. "Not a wife."

Lady Li did not respond but could not suppress her eyebrow from raising. What did Gong Furen expect? Lady Li was Lord Yun's wife; he could not have another.

"It is this matter of taking the girl to wife that has me the most concerned," Gong Furen said, trying to explain her position. "The girl has already been a concubine, and is past a suitable marriage age. My husband and I believe that taking Lady Swan as a concubine would be more appropriate. That way, after our son has grown more amiable to the idea of having a family of his own, he will still be able to take a wife later...A *Han* wife."

While it was generally looked down upon, it was not uncommon for a man to take a concubine before taking a wife. It was a way for a man to have the benefits of having a wife without the legal constraints of one, though it generally only happened among lower class people, such as men who could not afford a wife but hoped to buy one later. For Gong Furen to suggest that Swan be given to Inspector Gong as a concubine and not a first wife was a grave insult. Normally, a family as privileged as Lady Li's or Swan's would reject such an offer handily. But Swan had few other options. In fact, she had no other marriage prospects. So Lady Li once again pushed her anger deep into the pit of her stomach and forced a smile to her face.

"Lady Swan is the chaste widow of a great lord," Lady Li said. "She has everything she could ever need here in my home, and I value her company. I would not let her leave my home as anything less than a proper wife. Besides, I have spoken to Inspector Gong on this matter already, and he gave me his word that he would take Lady Swan as his wife. And I know how much he values his word."

Gong Furen's nostrils flared and she stared at Lady Li as though she could cow her with just a glance. But Lady Li did not budge. She did not show anger or fear. Her face was as emotionless as stone. Truly, she had nothing to gain or lose from the situation. Her only concern was doing the best she could by Swan, and right now, she wondered if calling off the match would be in Swan's best interest. She couldn't imagine being subjected to such an overbearing mother-in-law for the rest of her life. But she doubted Swan would ever thank her if she sabotaged her one chance at a new marriage.

Finally, Gong Furen stood, and her husband followed suit. "Thank you for your hospitality," she said with a slight bend of her knees, one not deep enough to show Lady Li the respect her station deserved, but just enough for Gong Furen to display her general dissatisfaction with the situation. "We will speak once more with our son and let you know if further arrangements are to be made."

Lady Li gave the Gongs a polite bend of her neck. Swan stood from her seat and then kneeled as low as she could on her pot-bottom shoes.

"I look forward to hearing from you soon," Lady Li said, and then motioned for Eunuch Bai, who had been standing silently to one side the whole time, to escort her guests out.

As soon as they were out of view, Lady Li collapsed back into her chair. "What an insufferable woman!" she said to Swan. "Are you sure you want to go through with this after meeting her?"

"I think it went rather well," Swan said, her face all smiles now that she didn't have to play the part of a humble servant.

"How can you think that?" Lady Li asked, kicking off her pot-bottom shoes and flexing her toes. "It was like haggling for fish at the market."

"But people only haggle over something they really want," Swan said as she snuck to the doorway to make sure they had completely gone. "They are just hoping you'll take a lower bride price, but they know they'll have to accept the match."

Lady Li shook her head, surprised by Swan's optimism and astuteness. "I think you may be right about that. If she wants Inspector Gong to marry, she'll have to accept you. He said he wouldn't marry anyone else."

Swan somehow managed to spin around on her tall shoes in a graceful twirl. "I can't believe I am finally going to be married again!"

Lady Li smiled but had to suppress a hint of her own sadness that tried to bubble up.

What she wouldn't give to be the one that Inspector Gong was wanting to marry.

She could never admit it out loud, though, of course. Unlike Swan, she simply wasn't in a position to marry. As a first wife, it was her duty to remain a chaste widow for the rest of her life. Even if she didn't care about that, she didn't want to hand over her immense wealth to a new husband and risk losing her daughters' dowries or compromise their status. As of right now, her oldest daughter was on the short list of possible consorts for the young emperor when he came of age. One day she could be the mother of the next empress of China! No, she couldn't marry. She had to stay the course that had been laid out for her.

"There is going to be so much to do!" Swan said, still dreaming of her wedding day. "I need to work on my embroidery. I still have many pieces in my trunk from my first marriage, but I am sure Mother Gong would appreciate some new ones. And I'll need a new wedding gown. Do you think Popo will let me take back the pots and cooking utensils I brought with me? And Mama and Baba will need new clothes as well. They will be so excited to know that I'm going to be a wife and not just a concubine anymore!"

She droned on as she went back to her own room with her wish list and things to do. There would actually be very little for Swan to do other than work on her embroidery. Weddings were always planned by the parents, and while

Lady Li wasn't her mother, she was her guardian, so much of the responsibility would fall to her. She groaned at the idea of having to plan a wedding with Gong Furen. Maybe she should reach out to Swan's mother and graciously offer her the chance to plan her daughter's second wedding.

"Mama! Mama!" her daughters cried out as they ran into the room waving a pamphlet in the air. They had just returned from visiting a nearby temple with Popo, their paternal grandmother.

Popo slowly passed by the room, leaning on her cane, but there was a smile on her face. Just a few short months ago, when Popo was living alone, she never had the strength to visit the temple, much less with her granddaughters in tow. While others might look at Popo and see a weak and frail woman, she was much improved from before.

"How was temple, Popo?" Lady Li asked.

"So many beggars!" Popo said with a shake of her head. "Hard times are upon us. Hard times, indeed."

Lady Li nodded as Popo went on past to her own quarters for a rest.

"What is this?" Lady Li asked as she returned her attention to her daughters as they fought over who got to climb up into her lap. Second Daughter won, though Lady Li thought that First Daughter must have let her win since she could have easily pushed her smaller sister out of the way.

"There is going to be a great opera performance tonight!" First Daughter said as she showed her mother the pamphlet. "Can we go!"

Lady Li opened the pamphlet and looked over the woodblock print of a Peking opera mask with information about the performance.

"'*The Concubine's Lover*,'" Lady Li read, "'will be performed at the White Lotus Theater tonight and feature the debut public performance by Wangshu in the role of the dan.' Huh, well isn't that something?"

"Everyone at temple was excited about it," First Daughter said, taking the pamphlet and turning it over in her hands. "What is so special about Wangshu?"

"Wangshu is a woman," Lady Li said. "Though you wouldn't know it by her name." She imagined the name had been specifically chosen by Wangshu for its ambiguous nature. "It says she is playing the dan, the female role. Quite novel, don't you think?"

"Women can perform in the opera?" Second Daughter asked, her mouth dramatically agape.

"The empress did decree that women could perform opera publicly now," Lady Li said as she gently closed her daughter's mouth. "It had been announced months ago, but I hadn't heard of any women taking to the stage until now. Wangshu has been performing in the empress's private imperial troop for years."

"I've never seen a woman in the opera before," First Daughter said dubiously, her eyebrow raised. She was already a little skeptic.

"Well, just because it was legal didn't mean anyone wanted to take the chance at being publicly ridiculed for it," Lady Li said. "It can be very hard to get people to try something new."

"Can we go?" Second Daughter asked. "I want to see!"

"Absolutely not!" Lady Li said, sliding her daughter off her lap as she stood. "A public opera house is no place for proper young ladies, and it will go well past your bedtime."

"Will you go?" First Daughter asked. "I heard several of the ladies at temple talking about going."

Lady Li ushered the girls toward the study to work on their reading lessons. "I haven't had time to think about it," she Li said. "I've been so preoccupied with helping Inspector Gong with the troubles in the legation and now negotiating Con—err, *Swan's* marriage."

First Daughter sighed. "You're always working."

"It's no easy task to run a house all by yourself," Lady Li scolded. "Just you wait until you have a family of your own."

First Daughter wrinkled her nose as if to argue, but then turned away. "Yes, mama," she said.

"What's wrong?" Lady Li asked, tugging on her daughter's sleeve.

The little girl shook her head. "Nothing. I know you want me to be empress."

"It would be a great honor," Lady Li said. "The most powerful woman in the country. Hundreds of servants. Countless beautiful gowns. Doesn't that sound lovely?"

"I suppose," First Daughter said, trying to turn away, but Lady Li held her fast.

"What is it?" she asked. "What's upsetting you?"

"I...I don't want to go to the palace to live," she finally admitted, her eyes downcast but brimming with tears.

Lady Li took her daughter in her arms. "What's all this? You know you must marry someday. Wouldn't it be best to marry an emperor?"

"But Auntie Suyi went to the palace and she came back dead!" First Daughter said sharply.

"I...I know," Lady Li said. "But that was an accident." It actually hadn't been an accident, but she didn't need to tell her daughters the brutal truth about that right now.

"And you went to the Forbidden City as a girl and you almost got killed too!" First Daughter went on.

"That...that was a very extreme circumstance," Lady Li tried to explain. She had, of course, told her daughters about her time at the Forbidden City many times, and about how she and the imperial family had been forced to flee by the invading foreigners. But she never imagined the story had instilled terror in her daughters. She had meant to inspire them with the empress's resilience at turning the invaders out and saving the throne for her young son.

"I don't want to go!" First Daughter said, stomping her foot.

Lady Li stood upright and looked down at her child. She wanted to help her cope with her emotions, but she couldn't let her think she could get her way by throwing a fit.

"You are a lady," Lady Li said. "And you do as you are told by your elders. If I decide that you are to go to the Forbidden City and marry the emperor, or go marry someone else, you will do it, do you understand?"

First daughter sucked in a breath and wiped her face with her long sleeves. "Yes, mama," she said.

"Good," Lady Li said. "Now, go clean your face and then come back to the study for your lesson."

First Daughter nodded as she headed to use the wash basin in her room. Lady Li then took Second Daughter by the hand and led her to the study room. Both girls did their lessons dutifully, but Lady Li could tell their hearts weren't in it. And truth be told, her mind was elsewhere as well. She hadn't realized how much the troubles of the court had upset her own children, and they had been shielded from the worst of it. Lady Li herself had been glad she was not chosen as an imperial consort. She was initially disappointed that her astrology chart did not align with the emperor's, so she was dismissed without even being considered. But after she ended up as a lady-in-waiting for the empress, she saw just how lonely and rigid her life was and was glad she had been spared such a life.

Yet, she still marched her daughter toward a fate she

had been so happy to escape. But what else could she do about it? Her daughters would have to marry eventually. Maybe they didn't have to marry the emperor, but any life with a husband would be one they couldn't control. Lady Li had never made a single decision in her life before the day her husband died.

"If Swan marries Gong Shushu," Second Daughter asked, "will we ever see her again?"

Lady Li felt a pain in her heart at the thought of never seeing Inspector Gong again, but she did her best not to let it show.

"I don't know," she replied. "Probably not. Swan has never returned to her parents' home since she came to live here. She has seen her mother a couple of times, but very rarely. Once she marries, we won't be her family anymore."

First Daughter grunted and crumpled up the page she was working on and threw it to the floor.

"I wish I'd been born a boy," First Daughter grumbled, trying her best not to cry.

"Why?" Lady Li asked, aghast.

"Because boys never have to leave their mothers."

The pain in Lady Li's heart was too great. She pulled both her daughters, her world, her reason for living, to her and held them tight.

"I will always be your mother," she whispered. "I will always be here for you."

After she kissed away her daughter's tears and comforted them as best she could, she sent them to their grandmother while she straightened up their books. The pamphlet for the opera slipped out from the papers and fluttered to the floor. She picked it up and read the introduction to Wangshu.

Daughter of the great opera performer Wangdi, Wangshu

was born with opera in her blood. As a performer for the empress, Wangshu has already achieved great heights. Yet she has agreed to descend to the world of mortals as the legendary Concubine Yu, who sacrificed all for love and duty.

Lady Li knew of some women who worked outside the home, but mostly they were the wives of tradesmen and laborers. Hardworking lower-class women who ran shops and served tea or sewed clothes. She had never considered that there could be a path through life that didn't involve marriage.

Of course, it would be ludicrous to think that her children might not marry but have some sort of career. But just for one night, maybe it wouldn't be so bad to dream about another life.

Maybe they could all use a night at the opera.

2

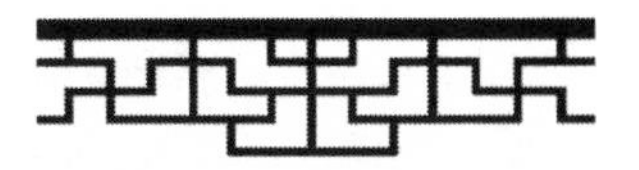

Inspector Gong apprehensively knocked on the door of Prince Kung's mansion. It had only been a few days since he had found out who killed the girl in the British Quarter, and the prince had been busy trying to calm the foreign powers who had been all too eager to declare war on China over the incident. He was sure the prince would not be in a kindly mood, yet his mother had refused to let him delay in speaking with the prince about getting an imperial dispensation to marry Swan. If he had to choose between an angry Prince Kung or an angry mother, Inspector Gong would choose the prince every time.

Only mere seconds after knocking, a servant opened the door and motioned for the inspector to enter. He was quickly ushered into a sitting room and offered a chair and tea, but he was too anxious to sit. He paced, admiring the many wall scrolls depicting mountains and rivers, swooping cranes, and galloping horses. Prince Kung loved art and culture and was a patron for many talented artists. His home was like a museum, housing countless relics and treasures from centuries of Chinese history.

"Enjoying my latest procurement, I see," Prince Kung said as he entered the room and caught Inspector Gong staring at a painting of a dancing woman. "It arrived while I was in endless meetings with Mr. Burlingame."

Inspector Gong raised an eyebrow. He kept the peace here at home while the prince dealt with the empire's international relations. He followed some of the news dealing with foreigners, but for the most part he ignored foreign issues.

"The Americans weren't involved in the threats against us after the girl died," Inspector Gong said. "Interesting that the US envoy would be meeting with you now."

"The vultures are always circling," Prince Kung said. "Looking for an opportunity to strike in a way that benefits them the most. But Burlingame's proposal is an interesting one. He wants to allow the Chinese to immigrate to America with no restrictions."

Inspector Gong scoffed. "The empress and magistrates can't be too happy about that. And how would it benefit the Americans?"

"They need workers," Prince Kung said as he sat in a chair and let out a long exhale. "American industry is exploding, and the American people are settling millions of li across the West. America has money and jobs but needs more people."

"Money. Jobs. People?" Inspection Gong said, finally calming enough to take a seat himself. "All things we need here in China."

Prince Kung nodded as he poured each of them a glass of baijiu. "Yes, but by allowing our people to go if they wish could earn us a lot of goodwill from the Americans. We need more allies in the world. Plus, maybe people who are...*dissatisfied* here would cause less trouble if they could just leave instead of rebelling."

Inspector Gong eyed the prince but kept his opinions to himself as he downed the harsh liquor. But the prince would not let his friend stay silent on the matter.

"What?" the prince prodded. "You do not agree?"

"You're dreaming if you think the people who are unhappy with Manchu rule are simply going to leave their homeland," Inspector Gong said bluntly.

"I am only trying to buy the empress time," the prince said into his glass. "She knows that changes must be made, changes my brother fought me on for years. If she can enact the modernizations we need, the Han may be less likely to continue their rebellions, at least for a few decades. Until the new emperor can take the throne. But we all know the days of the Qing Dynasty are numbered."

Inspector Gong had seen the prince despondent over the state of his country over the years. When they fought against rebels together in the western countryside. The day his father chose his brother over him to be the next emperor. The day the British burned the Summer Palace. But the prince had never given up. He had never stopped fighting to preserve the empire that his ancestors had forged. But there was now a weariness in the prince's eyes that Inspector Gong had not seen before. The prince was not old by any means, but a life of never-ending daily battles would take its toll on even the strongest of men.

"When one is riding a tiger, it can be hard to dismount," Inspector Gong said, reciting the common phrase to give his friend encouragement not to give up.

Prince Kung laughed. "And I thought I was the scholar."

"Hey, I had expensive tutors as well," Inspector Gong

said, pouring them each a new glass of baijiu. "Just don't let my mother find out that I remember anything I learned."

"How is she these days?" the prince asked as they clinked their glasses together and downed the drinks in one gulp.

Inspector Gong could already feel the alcohol warming his cheeks and making him lightheaded. "She's quite well. Rather busy these days. I…I've agreed to marry…finally."

"You old dog," Prince King said, slapping him on the back. "About time! Who is she?"

"That's why I'm here," Inspector Gong said. "She's Manchu. We need imperial permission to marry." It was against the law for a Han like Inspector Gong to marry a Manchu like Swan, but some exceptions could be made with high enough permission.

The prince's face dropped. "You know I would if I could," he said. "But Lady Li is too high ranking. You'd need permission from the empress, but even then—"

"It's not Lady Li," Inspector Gong interrupted. "It's her late husband's concubine, Swan."

"Swan?" the prince asked, confused. "You want to marry Swan?"

"Yes," Inspector Gong said firmly. "She proved to be quite an asset recently. We might not have found the killer in the legation without her help. I think she would make a capable wife."

"I don't doubt Swan's capability," the prince said. "But… you and Lady Li…does Swan know?"

The inspector wasn't sure just how dumb he should play. The prince knew that Inspector Gong and Lady Li had grown close, but whether he knew that they had actually been lovers, the inspector wasn't sure.

"I'm not sure what Swan knows," Inspector Gong admitted. "But Lady Li and I both agreed that Swan needs a new husband. And my mother is hell-bent on finding me a wife. This solves two problems at once."

"Do you know she's an opium addict?" the prince asked bluntly.

"I assumed as much when I found her in an opium den a few days ago," Inspector Gong said as though it was no big deal. "How did you know?"

"I know everything that goes on in Lady Li's home," the prince nearly yelled, but then he snapped his mouth shut and paced in a circle. He stuttered, as though he couldn't decide if he should laugh or be angry.

Inspector Gong knew that many years before, back when Lady Li was a lady-in-waiting at the Forbidden City, before she was married, she and the prince had been in love and hoped to marry. But circumstance kept them apart, and she ended up married to someone else. The inspector knew that the prince and Lady Li were no longer lovers, but they had remained close friends. At the prince's outburst, he couldn't help but wonder, and not for the first time, if there was more to their current relationship than he thought.

"This is ludicrous," the prince finally settled on. "You've been sleeping with Lady Li yet you're taking her opium eating slave to wife? Not just as a concubine, which you wouldn't need my permission for. Have you completely lost your senses? What does your mother think?"

"My mother can be surprisingly open-minded when she wants something badly enough," Inspector Gong said.

"Does she know Swan is addicted to opium?" the prince asked.

Inspector Gong sighed and dropped his arms. "No, she does not. But Lady Li is keeping Swan confined and watched at all times so she can't access it anymore. By the time we marry, I'm certain her addiction will be broken."

"You and I have both seen the effects of opium on our people," the prince said darkly. "You know it is not that simple."

"Are you going to give me permission to marry Swan or not?" the inspector asked.

"I'd rather marry her myself if it kept you from doing something this stupid," the prince grumbled.

"I'd marry Lady Li if I could," Inspector Gong said. "I've all but formally asked her. But you know we can't. She won't. There's too much at risk for her. But Swan is the next best thing. She's smart, beautiful, still young. If I'd never met Lady Li, I'd think there was no woman better for me than Swan."

"But you *have* met Lady Li," the prince said. "Can you really care for Swan the way she deserves when all of us know what you really want?"

"All I can do is try," the inspector said, the words coming out more defeated than he meant. "Lady Li, Swan, my mother, and I have all agreed to the arrangement. All we need is your permission to see it through. If I didn't want this, I could have just told them that you refused without ever really asking you. I'm here because I *want* your permission. Prince Kung, will you give me leave to marry Yun Swan?"

The prince rolled his eyes and scoffed. "Well, who am I to prevent you from making the biggest mistake of your life?"

Inspector Gong gave the prince the fist-in-palm salute and bowed. "Thank you."

"I'll have the paper drawn up and stamped tomorrow," the prince said. "But for now, I need a break from all this madness. I'm going to the opera. Want to accompany me? My wife, Guwalgiya, will be accompanying me."

"The highest-ranking man in the country and his wife attending a public opera?" Inspector Gong asked. "How scandalous."

The prince picked up a pamphlet from a table and handed it to him. "It's the first public opera in Peking to feature a woman in the role of the dan."

"Is it?" Inspector Gong asked, intrigued, as he skimmed the pamphlet. "The empress made it legal for women to be actors months ago, didn't she?"

"She did," the prince said. "But no women have dared to do so, or their opera troops have not allowed them to. Bucking social order is not something the people eagerly accept."

"So what made this Wangshu decide to take the risk?" the inspector asked.

"She has been performing in the empress's private troop for years," the prince explained. "I've seen her perform many times. She's quite talented. Comes from a long line of performers. But when the empress realized that there were no women willing to step into the role of the dan after she gave them permission, she asked Wangshu to set the example."

"Why does the empress care so much?" the inspector asked. "She can have whoever she wants to perform in her private troop."

"The empress and I have been working together for a long time," the prince said, which was rather an understatement. The empress was only ruling China because she and the prince—with the help of Lady Li—had overthrown the men that the last emperor had selected to be the new emperor's guardian until he came of age. After a lifetime of faithful service, the emperor had completely pushed Prince Kung out of his son's future government. The empress and Prince Kung knew that the Qing Dynasty would fall immediately if that happened, so they had the new regents exiled or executed and set the empress up to rule on her son's behalf with Prince Kung as her chief advisor.

"The empress wants to make changes," the prince went on. "She wants to modernize the country, but she has to be careful. Move slowly. Too many changes too quickly will spook the ministers and the people. Allowing women to perform in the opera is her small way of embarking on social change. She wants this first tiny change to be a success."

"Sounds like more trouble than it's worth," the inspector said, handing the pamphlet back. "I think I'll stay home for once."

"I'd rather you went," the prince said. "I'm going to support Wangshu and the empress, and to set an example for the other nobles. But Wangshu has been receiving threatening letters. People have been harassing her on the street. She's worried about her safety. I told her she didn't need to worry, but I'd feel more confident if you were there tonight."

"So now I'm to play bodyguard for an actress?" Inspector Gong asked, wrinkling his nose. "Sounds like a dreadful way to spend an evening."

The prince sighed. "It would certainly be a shame if something were to happen to her and I ended up too busy to get that marriage dispensation for you."

"Where's my ticket?" Inspector Gong asked.

3

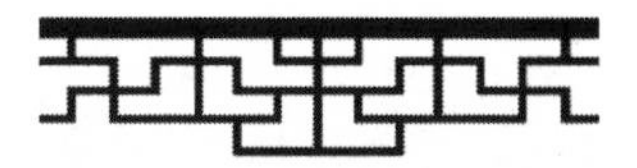

First Daughter and Second Daughter were nearly bouncing with excitement in the sedan chair as the chair-bearers carried the girls and Lady Li to the theater.

"I can't wait to see the costumes!" First Daughter said as she tried to peek through the tied curtains of the sedan chair.

"The singing! The dancing!" Second Daughter exclaimed as she tried to move her sister out of the way so she could see out.

"Calm down, girls," Lady Li chided. "You make it harder for the boys to carry us with you moving back and forth."

"The sword fighting!" First Daughter said, not hearing her mother. "Just like Mongeyisu!" They both then devolved into a fit of laughter. They loved pretending they were Mongeyisu, the Manchu heroine of myth and legend.

"Girls, please!" Lady Li tried again, physically forcing them to their seats. "You must sit down! I can have the boys take you right back home where you can sit in your rooms like Swan!"

That got the girls' attention, and they quickly sat, with their hands folded in their laps, but their feet continued to wiggle.

"Why couldn't Swan come, mama?" First Daughter asked.

"It wouldn't be proper for a betrothed woman to be seen in public," Lady Li said, which both was and was not true. Had Swan been never married, it would be inappropriate for her to be out in public where other men can see her. As a widow, however, there were no rules about her being seen in public as long as she was properly supervised. She had left strict instructions with the staff to make sure that Swan didn't leave her room and that no one was to deliver her anything other than food from the kitchen. Everyone knew that Swan's marriage depended on breaking her opium addiction. And while Swan herself wanted to come out of the cloud and marry Inspector Gong, Lady Li knew that the mere thought of having a bit of opium could break the resolve of the strongest person.

She wished she could have left Eunuch Bai behind. He was the only person she really trusted with her household in her absence. But as a woman herself, she shouldn't be seen at a public event without a male escort, so he was with her, trotting along outside the sedan chair with the chair-bearers.

Lady Li rubbed her forehead and tried to forget all her troubles, just for one night. She needed the break, the escape from the world. She was looking forward to the opera and hoped it would provide her with a well-deserved distraction.

The White Lotus Theater was a bustle of activity. Men and women of every social standing were in attendance. Some people were trying to get into the theater while others were just milling about outside. Some people were hawking their wares, including some women who were offering their services.

"How can you support this abomination!" one man screamed at Lady Li as she exited the sedan chair. "You should be contained to your own house! Women should be kept behind silk screens!"

Lady Li looked around and saw several angry faces chiding the people who were trying to enter. She hadn't expected to see protesters here. She nearly climbed back into her chair, afraid for her children's safety, when she felt Eunuch Bai's hand on her arm.

"This way, my lady," he said. Of course, he would know a quick and safe way inside. Lady Li carried Second Daughter and held First Daughter's hand tightly as they worked their way through the crowd and into the building.

The crowd inside was not much thinner. The show was oversold. She could see the elevated stage at the back of the large open-air courtyard, but there were far more people than benches. Not that it mattered since most people who had bench seats would stand anyway to get a better view.

Eunuch Bai led Lady Li to a stairwell that would lead to boxed seats on the second level.

"Inspector Gong!" Lady Li exclaimed in surprise when Eunuch Bai opened the sliding door to the room and she saw him standing there. "What are you doing here?"

"Not happy to see me?" he asked as he gave a small bow and smile.

Lady Li felt a tightness and a fluttering in her chest at the same time. She was more than happy to see him, but disappointed that they could never be more than mere acquaintances. And here, in front of so many people, they would have to be on the most formal of terms.

"I did not expect to see you here," she finally managed to say.

Second Daughter squirmed out of her arms and ran to hug him. "Gong Shushu!" she cried out, jumping up to give him a hug. Even since the girls learned that he would be marrying Swan, they had taken to calling him uncle.

He hugged her and gave her a kiss on the forehead. "I can't believe your mama let you out of the house so late at night."

"Children need fresh air sometimes," Lady Li said.

He looked around Lady Li as if checking to see if anyone else was with her. "Is Swan with you?" he asked, and Lady Li hoped that her heart sinking like a rock did not show on her face.

"It is a good thing I didn't," she said, pushing past him further into the room. "You know you aren't supposed to speak with her before the wedding." She then realized that Inspector Gong must have come as a guest of Prince Kung, who was standing near the edge of the balcony with his wife. Lady Li approached them and bowed.

"My prince," she said. "My lady."

Lady Guwalgiya gave Lady Li a polite nod, but then turned away to speak to her own friends. Lady Li and Lady Guwalgiya had never gotten along. The prince had been married to Lady Guwalgiya when he was very young, only fifteen years old, as was common for imperial children. So the prince had already been married for nearly a decade by the time he and Lady Li met and fallen in love, carrying on an affair within the walls of the Forbidden City. Lady Li had no idea how much Lady Guwalgiya knew about the affair, but she clearly knew enough to treat Lady Li cordially—as was appropriate for their stations—but kept her at a cool distance.

The prince took Lady Li's hand in his and held it warmly. "It is a pleasure to see you."

"And you, dear friend," Lady Li said, and she meant it. Even though she had at one time loved him and would have settled for being a concubine herself to be with him, it meant a lot to her to still be able to count him among her friends. He was one of the few people she knew she could still count on in a crisis.

"Our mutual friend came to my home and made a rather unusual request today," the prince said, eyeing Inspector Gong.

"Oh?" she asked.

"I have no reason to deny him other than I think it is a stupid idea," he said. "But he said you had given him and Swan your full approval. Is this true? I would never do anything to make you unhappy."

"Is it possible I both approve this thing and it makes me unhappy?" she asked as she stepped over to the railing and looked down at the crowd below. She and the prince had a shared history so deep, there was no need to be coy.

"Then why are you doing it?" the prince asked. "Just carry on as you have. Take him to your bed if you must, but don't yolk Swan's misfortunes to him. To his family."

"But I can't," Lady Li said. "It...it's not so simple. I have to let him go."

"By the gods," the prince said, somewhere between shock and amusement. "You love the bastard, don't you? That's why you can't just sleep with him and go about your life."

Lady Li didn't respond, but she gripped the railing so hard she thought it would shatter.

"Well, I am sorry for it," the prince said. "I have loved

many women, but only been in love once. I know how hard it is to have to let that person go."

She looked up into his eyes and saw all of their stolen kisses and hidden trysts in the Forbidden City pass by.

"But we became better people for it," Lady Li said. "We both lived full lives, have beautiful families. We have been better friends than lovers."

"But it's different with him, is it?" the prince asked. "With me, we were young and there were no consequences if we'd been caught. But with him, there's a lot at stake. You've been willing to risk everything to be with him."

"And that's why he has to go," she said. "I can't have him around. I need him safely married and out of my life."

"If you wanted him well and truly out of your life you'd have him marry anyone else but Swan," he said.

The orchestra started banging the drums and clashing the cymbals, starting the show.

"Just sign the damn paper," Lady Li snapped as she took a seat and pulled her daughters close to her.

The prince sighed and went to the end of the row to sit with his wife.

"Mama, what's happening?" First Daughter asked as the opera performers appeared on stage, one wearing the head of a horse, and one wearing the head of a bull. They were both twirling long spears.

"Horse Head and Ox Head are guardians of the gates of hell," Lady Li said.

Inspector Gong sat next to Lady Li and took Second Daughter into his lap. "As long as you are explaining what is going on," he said, "I might as well sit here and listen as well or else I'll be completely lost."

Lady Li frowned at him, but then felt the anger and annoyance melt away and she gave him a small smile. He slid closer to her, so close their arms were touching, and she did not move away.

Several more actors came out and performed an acrobatic routine.

"Those are demons," Lady Li explained.

The demons were supposed to be frightening, but First Daughter and Second Daughter found the flips and tricks hilarious.

Then a man dressed all in red with a long beard came out. His face was painted in gold and white.

"That's the Laosheng," Lady Li said. "The man of reason and decency. He is also the King of Hell."

The King of Hell sang a long solo and marched around the stage.

"He is explaining that war has been raging for many years," Lady Li said. "Sending many good men to hell."

The King of Hell and the demons then performed several songs and had many discussions about what to do about the never-ending war in the mortal realm. The songs were long, as it was common for opera performances to take a whole day, but this one had been cut down to last only a few hours.

Finally, the King of Hell called his daughter forth, and everyone in the audience held their breath.

In a long blue gown embroidered with silver thread and sparkling silver jewels and long white sleeves, Wangshu walked on stage with such small steps she seemed to float across the stage.

The cymbals crashed and the audience broke out in cheers and jeers. Wangshu moved to the middle of the stage with practiced precision. Every movement of her head, every flick of her wrist was deliberate and held meaning. After a moment, it was clear the crowd was not going to quiet, so Wangshu opened her mouth and went on with the show.

In a clear and high-pitched voice, Wangshu, playing the role of Xueyan, the immortal daughter of the King of Hell who would give up her eternal life to stop a great war by becoming the Red Concubine to one of the generals fighting the war, silenced the audience.

Even Lady Li stopped narrating the show because she was so entranced by the performance and didn't want to miss a beat.

At the end of the play, everyone was on the edge of their seat as Xueyan realized that the only way to end the war is to kill the human general she had fallen in love with.

Xueyan, now dressed in red as befitting the act she was about to perform, sang a song lamenting her tragic fate. She knew that by killing her lover, she would complete the task her father assigned to her, but she hopes that when she returns to hell, he tortures her forever instead of celebrating her victory because she knows she will not be able to live with herself after she completes the task.

Lady Li was not the only person in the audience trying to discreetly wipe away tears. First Daughter had long fallen asleep despite the loudness of the show. But Second Daughter was riveted, watching every moment with rapt attention.

The audience went completely silent as Xueyan hid a sword under her gown and the general entered the stage. Lady Li was surprised by the casting of the general. He was good-looking, even under layers of makeup, but he had a slight build, not the muscular body of someone who usually took on such a role. But he still played the role perfectly, convincingly playing both Xueyan's tender lover and a merciless warmonger.

Together, the general and Xueyan sang a song about how much they loved each other and would run away and live in peace if only the war would ever end. But then the general broke away from her and sang about how the war could never end, not until he wiped the barbarians off the face of the earth.

Xueyan wept bitterly at the general's words because she knew she had no choice but to kill him. She stepped behind the general and drew her sword. But she wouldn't stab him in the back. He turned to her and embraced her, kissing her passionately.

Then the general gasped. He stumbled back, looking down at the sword in his stomach in shock. He grabbed Xueyan's shoulder, and she looked just as terrified as he did.

"What...what have you done?" the general asked as he fell backward off the sword, which was still tightly gripped in Xueyan's hand.

Lady Li was surprised that the general did not sing his final words, but the power of the scene could not be denied. Xueyan's sword and sleeves were drenched in blood, an effect Lady Li had not seen at an opera before.

Everyone in the audience held their breath as they waited for Xueyan's response to the act she just committed, but the song never came.

Wangshu simply stared out at the crowd, her hand holding the bloody sword shaking. Then she ran off stage. The crowd started murmuring.

Lady Li felt Inspector Gong grip her hand.

"What...what is happening?" she asked.

"I'm no expert on opera," he said. "But I think Wangshu just killed her co-star."

4

Like most people, Inspector Gong had seen operas before, but he was hardly a connoisseur. In fact, before the dramatic murder of the general, he had hardly been paying attention at all. All of his thoughts had been on Lady Li, who was sitting closely beside him.

He was always pleasantly surprised by how naturally they seemed to fit together. As they watched the show, side by side, and the evening grew progressively darker, he slipped his hand into hers, and she did not pull away. In fact, she held his hand tightly and even moved closer to him until they were sitting shoulder to shoulder. Enjoying an opera under the stars, hand in hand, with her children and their friends, Inspector Gong couldn't imagine a more perfect night out. Any thoughts of Swan had completely vanished as he once again dreamed of a life with Lady Li. A life they both knew could never happen, yet they couldn't seem to completely let go of.

Eventually, though, he found his attention drawn to the opera performance. Wangshu had a beautiful voice and was a gifted actress. The character of Xueyan was supposed to stop the war by any means necessary. Her original plan had been to merely seduce and distract the general and convince him to return home and stop the fighting. But she found herself falling in love with him instead. She also understood his reasons for the rebellion. The emperor had been dealing cruelly with his people. Xueyan was conflicted, caught between her heart and her honor.

Inspector Gong knew all too well the emotions coursing through Xueyan as the opera progressed. He wondered if Lady Li saw the similarities between the play and their real life. Who was he kidding? Of course, she did. Lady Li was one of the most well-educated and clever women he knew. He looked forward to discussing the opera with her after it ended, if she would speak to him. But that was what he wanted from a wife. Not merely a bedmate, but a friend, a partner. Someone he could talk to at the end of a long day.

He supposed Swan could provide that as well. Lord Yun would have only chosen the best quality woman to be his concubine. But it didn't matter if Swan was Lady Li's equal in every way. She still wasn't Lady Li, the woman he was in love with and truly wanted.

He was a fool for agreeing to marry Swan. He was only going to break her heart and be a disappointment to her. He knew it. But what could he do about it? He had already agreed and asked the prince for the dispensation. There was no going back.

He was starting to panic, feeling trapped, when the opera came to its dramatic climax.

Xueyan had come to the realization that she had to kill the general. There was no other way to stop the war. As the general kissed her one last time, Xueyan drew her sword and plunged it into his stomach. Everyone in the audience gasped at the scene, some people even crying.

But as Inspector Gong saw the blood pooling under the dead general, he knew the man's death had not been an act.

He stood up and rushed from the booth.

"Inspector!" he heard Lady Li call to him. "Where are you going?"

But he did not have time to reply. Wangshu had fled from the stage; he couldn't let her escape the theater.

As he reached the first floor, the crowd seemed confused. Some were standing and clapping while others were still sitting and murmuring. People who were familiar with the show knew there were still several more scenes to come. And the fact that the general was still lying on the stage in an ever-growing puddle of his own blood was a hint that the show had not gone according to plan.

The Lord of Hell appeared on stage and started his next song. Inspector Gong couldn't understand all of the words, but the actor must have been trying to convince the audience that all was well and the show was continuing as normal. It wouldn't work. They couldn't leave the actor there for another hour. But it was better than letting on that something had happened. The last thing the inspector needed right now was a riot.

He let the Lord of Hell provide the distraction for the audience while he made his way backstage. He was surprised that there were no guards to keep people from coming and going as they wished. He hoped that Wangshu had not already escaped.

He grabbed the arm of the first actor he came across. "Where is Wangshu?" he demanded.

He could feel the young man trembling. "Her...her dressing room," he said, pointing down a long hallway with a shaky finger.

"You need to come up with a convincing way to end this show," the inspector said. "And get the audience out."

"B-b-but..." the man stuttered. "How? There is much story left to tell! The general is supposed to have his scene in hell and Xueyan's own death and..."

"I don't care how you do it!" the inspector snapped, pushing the man out of his way. "Just end it before everyone learns they just witnessed a murder."

Inspector Gong heard the boy whimper before running off as he marched toward the dressing room. He turned the doorknob, but it was locked.

"Wangshu!" he called. "Open this door."

He could hear someone rummaging around inside, but the door didn't open.

"Open this door or I will break it down!" the inspector yelled. He heard a yelp from inside and something shatter. He stood back and kicked at the door, which was quite flimsy and fell open with ease.

As he stepped into the room, he saw that the room was a disaster. Clothes and other items were strewn about, most streaked with blood. There was a traveling case open on a table, filled with bloody clothes. A hand mirror lay shattered on the floor.

Wangshu turned toward the inspector, still gripping the bloody sword in one hand.

"Wangshu," he said, holding his hand out. "Give me the sword."

She gasped and tears ran down her face. "I...I didn't do it," she cried, her makeup smearing down her face.

"I know," the inspector said, taking a step toward her, his hand still outstretched. Of course, she had done it. Hundreds of people had just seen her run her co-star through with the bloody sword in her hand. But he would say whatever it took to calm her down and get her to cooperate. "Just give me the sword."

She looked down at her hands and gasped, as if she hadn't realized she was still holding the murder weapon.

"Oh!" she cried as she reached up and rubbed her temple, smearing blood along her face. "Fanhua! It was just an act. All part of the show. He's...he's just fine, isn't he?"

Fanhua, that was the name of the actor playing the general, the man who was now dead on stage. Inspector Gong remembered seeing the name in the pamphlet.

"Everything will be fine," the inspector said, still inching toward her. "But you need to give me the sword."

"No," she said firmly. "I can't. It's not my sword."

"Then whose sword is it?" the inspector asked, wondering just how much of what Wangshu was saying was lucid and how much was from shock.

She shook her head and started to pace. "I don't know," she said. "But they will come for it. Someone will come for it. I can't let it go."

This was interesting information, the inspector thought. Perhaps someone had hired her or forced her to kill Fanhua.

"I am Inspector Gong," he said. "The head of Prince Kung's police force. I will find out who the sword belongs to, but I need you to give it to me."

Wangshu stared at him, squeezing the hilt of the sword she held in front of her. They stood silently, at an impasse.

"Wangshu!" the young man the inspector had accosted in the hall earlier yelled as he burst into the room. "The crowd is growing restless. They refuse to believe the show is over or leave. We need you to come back and sing your last song."

"Are you kidding?" Inspector Gong hissed at the man. "She just killed someone. I have to arrest her."

"But...the audience..." the man stuttered.

Inspector Gong stepped out of Wangshu's room and peeked around the wall to the stage and the crowd beyond it. He had been so focused on catching Wangshu he hadn't thought about the hundreds of patrons who were assembled only feet from the victim. He looked at the dead body of Fanhua and then at the people who were standing at the edge of the stage within arm's length. How they hadn't figured out that Fanhua was dead was beyond him. But he supposed that was the power of the man's performance.

He then realized the audience was rather a large problem. They could easily storm the stage, corrupt the murder scene, even steal the body if they wanted to. They could riot or turn on Wangshu. If the audience realized the truth, all of the actors could be in real danger.

They needed to end the show and dismiss the crowd without incident before he could actually deal with the crime that had taken place. He couldn't believe what he was about to say, but he didn't think he had a choice.

"Wangshu," he said, stepping back into her room. "You need to go out and sing your last song. You need to end the show and send the patrons away. Do you think you can do that?"

He didn't think she could. She looked like a terrified leaf, trembling in the wind. But at the mention of going back on stage, a surreal calmness seemed to wash over her.

"I can do it," she said. She held up her head and walked toward the door.

Inspector Gong stopped her, reaching for the sword. "I need you to give that to me."

She shook her head. "I can't," she said. "I need it for the final act."

Inspector Gong pressed his lip. *Actors!* "Fine," he said. "But if you try to hurt anyone else with it, I will stop you myself."

She gave a small nod and moved toward the edge of the stage. Inspector Gong knew it was crazy to let her go back out there, back to the scene of the crime, holding the murder weapon, out of his grasp where she could try to flee, but he wasn't sure he had another choice. He needed some way to clear the audience.

As she stepped onto the stage, the Lord of Hell froze, and if not for the layer of makeup he was wearing, Inspector Gong would have sworn the man's face blanched. He backed up and then fled from the stage. He probably thought that Wangshu had come to kill him as well.

But instead, Wangshu slipped back into the role of Xueyan, the woman who had saved the world by killing her lover. She walked over to the body of the general and wept. Then she opened her mouth to sing her final song.

She sang about how unfair the world was for women—both the mortal world and the underworld. How to be a filial daughter to the King of Hell she had to betray her heart and her lover. How she had to be subject to the emperor even though she knew he had acted wrongly. How she had to betray her own heart to fulfill the expectations placed on her. How the only way she could avoid having to live in the underworld with what she had done for all of eternity she would have to cut out her own heart.

Inspector Gong gasped as he listened to her words. He hadn't considered that she would hurt *herself* with the sword. Dammit! He shouldn't have let her return to the stage. But what could he do now? If he ran out there and stopped her, the audience would know that something terrible had happened—or was about to happen—and he had no idea how they would react. They most certainly wouldn't leave the theater quickly, easily, or orderly.

He glanced up at the box where Lady Li and Prince Kung were. They were still in the box, but they were not sitting. They were both crowded in the front corner, watching intently, talking heatedly. They both knew that something terrible had happened, but they didn't know what to do about it either. They probably thought that Inspector Gong had already captured Wangshu and were shocked when she came back on stage. He waved at them from the edge of the stage, trying to tell them that he had everything under control.

But he had nothing under control. He had no idea what Wangshu was going to do or how to stop her. All he could do was watch.

Wangshu continued singing about her plan to end her own life so she could be with the general for eternity. She raised the sword, which was still stained with the General's blood.

She then plunged the sword into her chest and fell backward onto the stage. Several people in the audience cried out in shock.

Then they erupted into cheers.

5

Lady Li gasped as Wangshu plunged the sword into her own chest. Where was Inspector Gong? How could he have let Wangshu return to the stage? She had just killed the actor who had been playing the general. He was still there on the stage, the blood growing dark. This was no act. And now was Wangshu dead as well? She seemed to have been in shock after the general fell to the floor. How could she then do the same thing to herself? It didn't make sense.

Prince Kung turned to exit the box.

"Where are you going?" Lady Li asked, gripping his arm.

"To send for my guards so they can dismiss the audience quickly," he said. "Something has gone wrong. We need these people out of here."

"But the guards could make it worse," she said. "They could cause a panic. Right now, the audience seems oblivious to what they have just witnessed."

"But when the general doesn't get up for his final bow," the prince said, pulling away from her and stepping out of the room, "they will know it wasn't an act."

"What can I do to help?" Lady Li called after him.

"I'm not sure," he said. "Go backstage and see if Inspector Gong needs your assistance."

Lady Li nodded. She wasn't sure how she could help, but she felt she needed to do something. She was glad the prince hadn't simply dismissed her and ordered her to go home.

She motioned Eunuch Bai to her side. His wide eyes told her that he had not missed any of her words to the prince and that he knew exactly what was going on. "Take the girls home right now," she said.

"But what about you, mistress?" he asked, alarmed. "Surely it would be safer if you came home as well."

"I don't know what's going on, but I can't leave just yet. I need to find out what happened to Wangshu," she reasoned. "Take the girls home and then send the sedan chair back for me. I'll come home as soon as I can."

Eunuch Bai wrinkled his nose, as though they both knew she wouldn't be returning home anytime soon, but he knew better than to say anything. He simply gave a bow and then picked up First Daughter, who had slumped over and was soundly sleeping on the hard bench. He then took Second Daughter by the hand and pulled her away.

"But I want to stay," Second Daughter begged, trying to pull her hand from Eunuch Bai's grasp. "Can we go backstage and meet Wangshu?"

"Not tonight, darling," Lady Li said. "It's too late."

Second Daughter groaned her unhappiness, but she let Eunuch Bai lead her away.

Lady Li went down the stairs and started to work her way through the crowd. The people were still clapping, talking, milling about, waiting for something else to happen. No one seemed to be trying to leave.

Finally, the crowd erupted into cheers again. Lady Li strained her neck to see what had everyone so excited and saw Wangshu stand up and bow to the crowd. She then waved to the sidelines and several of the other actors came out as well and they all bowed together. But the general still laid there dead.

Wangshu stepped forward and addressed the crowd. "I'm afraid that Fanhua is committed to his role and will not stand up until after everyone leaves," she said with a laugh. The audience laughed along with her. She shot a pointed look to The Lord of Hell.

He tossed his head back and let out a jolly belly laugh. "Perhaps I should have Horse Head and Ox Head drag him to the underworld."

The audience cheered their agreement, but Wangshu playfully slapped his arm.

"That would be so rude," she said. "I'm sure he will come backstage with us as soon as everyone stops looking at him."

At that, all the doors to the theater were thrown open and Prince Kung's guards started to usher everyone out.

A few drunken patrons tried to be belligerent, but for the most part, everyone filed out in an orderly manner. Except for Lady Li. When the crowd had thinned enough, she made her way backstage.

She found Inspector Gong just as the actors also made their way backstage.

The Lord of Hell grabbed Wangshu's arm and spun her to face him. "What have you done?" he yelled in her face, shaking her vigorously.

Wangshu dropped her sword, and it clattered to the floor. She started to cry and moved to put her hands to her face, but she froze, as though seeing the blood on them for the first time and started screaming.

The Lord of Hell slapped her so hard, her neck snapped to the side and she fell to the floor.

Inspector Gong stepped forward and restrained the Lord of Hell. "That's enough," he said. "She's in shock."

Lady Li ran to Wangshu's side. "Are you all right?" she asked. "What happened?"

Wangshu sat up and held her hand, the blood upon which was brown and dry, to her cheek and she continued to cry. "I don't know. I don't know," she mumbled as she started to rock.

Inspector Gong checked to make sure the audience had been cleared out.

"Hey! Get away from there," he yelled to two of the other actors who were hovering around the dead general's body.

Wangshu looked in his direction and then cried out when she saw the body. Lady Li took her by the arm and turned her so she didn't have to face it.

"Wangshu," Lady Li said, looking into her eyes. "Do you remember me? I was a lady-in-waiting for the empress. I'm Lady Li."

Wangshu looked at Lady Li for a moment, her brow scrunched, then she nodded. She sniffed, but her wailing had stopped. Lady Li rubbed her shoulder.

"Good," she said. "Now can you tell me what happened?"

Wangshu used one of her long, draping sleeves to rub her face, smearing her perfect makeup. "The sword..." she said, glancing to where it still lay on the floor. "It...it's just a prop. The blade is supposed to fold into the handle..." She shook her head in disbelief. "But it didn't. It just...it went in and…" She held her hand to her mouth as she started to gag.

Lady Li shook her gently to get her attention. "Don't do that," she said. "I need you to stay strong for me, okay?"

Inspector Gong walked over to the sword and picked it up by the hilt. He tested the blade against a wooden beam. It did not collapse as Wangshu had described.

"It's a real sword," he said, and the other actors gasped. He turned to the Lord of Hell. "What do you say? Was it supposed to be a fake sword?"

The Lord of Hell nodded. "All the weapons we use are merely imitation." He went over and grabbed a lance. As he shook it, the blade quivered. "Real weapons would be too heavy or dangerous to use while on stage."

Inspector Gong handed the sword to the Lord of Hell. "Shouldn't the girl have noticed if this sword was heavier than usual?"

The Lord of Hell hesitated as he eyed the blood on the blade, but then he took it and bounced it in his hand. "This is a rather light sword, so it is similar in weight to the prop she should have used. The prop sword is more durable because it has to look like it is really entering the body, but as she said, it should have collapsed when pressed firmly against Fanhua's body. But this looks nothing like the prop sword. The design on the hilt is completely different."

"We only rehearsed the play once," Wangshu said. "I didn't memorize what the stupid sword looked like."

"So this is your story?" the inspector asked Wangshu. "That the sword was switched so you killed him by accident?"

"It's not a story," she said. "It's the truth! I would never kill someone!"

"But you *did* kill someone," the inspector said. "Accident

or not, *you* ran him through with your own hand. And there are hundreds of witnesses."

Wangshu stood up and backed away from the inspector. "But I didn't do it!" she said. "I mean...I...I didn't try to. I didn't..."

"I know what you mean," the inspector said as he walked slowly toward her. "But you are still a murderess and I'm going to have to arrest you."

"No!" she gasped, turning away and trying to flee, but Lady Li stood in her path. "Lady Li," Wangshu begged. "Don't let him do this. It was an accident."

Lady Li sympathized with Wangshu. She did not think that the girl was a cold-hearted killer. But she didn't think there was anything she could do. "I'm so sorry," Lady Li said.

Inspector Gong grabbed Wangshu by the arm.

"No! Stop!" she screamed as she tried to pull away, her tears starting up again.

"What's going on?" Prince Kung demanded, walking up the aisle and hopping up onto the stage.

"I'm arresting Wangshu for the murder of Fanhua," the inspector declared. "There might be more to the case, and I'll look into it, but there is no denying that she killed the man."

"What do you mean more to the case?" the prince asked, crossing his arms.

Inspector Gong released Wangshu and took the sword from the Lord of Hell, handing it to the prince. "She says that the sword was switched. She thought she was using just a prop sword, a collapsible one, but she was actually holding this one. She says the death was an accident."

The prince tested the blade. "And do you believe her?" he asked the inspector.

"I don't know yet," the inspector said. "And I'm not sure her intentions matter. Either way, the man ended up dead at her hand."

Wangshu grunted in frustration. "But I didn't do it!" she said, stomping her foot. "Someone switched the sword! That person should be arrested, not me!"

"Who do you think switched the sword?" the inspector asked.

"I...I don't know," she said, holding up her hands, which were covered with her long sleeves, helplessly.

"Why would someone switch them?" the inspector pressed. "Who would want Fanhua dead?"

"*You're* the inspector," Wangshu spat. "You should be finding out instead of arresting me."

The inspector stepped forward, gripping her arm roughly. Lady Li placed her hand on his arm to still his anger.

"That's enough, both of you," she said, using a tone typically reserved for her children. She then turned her attention to Inspector Gong. "There must be something you can do to help her."

"Help a murderer?" he asked. "You saw her kill the man just as I did."

"But these are extreme circumstances," Lady Li said. "If you only arrest her, you could be letting the real killer, a very dangerous and brazen one, go free."

"I said I would look into the switching of the blade," Inspector Gong said. "But I still need to arrest Wangshu."

"But if you arrest her, the Ministry of Justice might put her death in a matter of days!" Lady Li finally said bluntly. She didn't want to scare Wangshu further, or give her cause to run, but Inspector Gong was ignoring the fact that once he took her in, what happened next was beyond his control.

"What?" Wangshu yelled, her face going pale even under her smeared makeup. "But...but...I—"

"I know," Inspector Gong said, interrupting her and rolling his eyes. "You didn't do it."

"Well, I didn't," she said through gritted teeth.

"Enough," the prince said stepping forward. Everyone silenced. "This is a serious matter. But there is a lot more going on here. While Wangshu should be held accountable for her crime in some way—"

Wangshu gasped but quickly shut her mouth when the prince looked at her.

"There is most likely a far more sinister, and possibly more dangerous, killer on the loose," the prince continued. "For now, Wangshu will not be arrested, but one of my guards will watch her to make sure she doesn't escape. In the meantime, Inspector Gong will look for whoever switched the blade and find out what is really going on here."

"Yes, your highness," Inspector Gong said as he dropped Wangshu's arm, which she then rubbed dramatically.

"All of you," the prince said looking at the various actors. "Are to cooperate with the inspector's investigation. Do you understand?"

"Yes, your highness," they all said with a bow.

The prince then turned away and ordered someone to bring a sheet to cover Fanhua's body. The inspector went over to talk to him.

"That inspector has it out for me," Wangshu whispered to Lady Li. "He won't be satisfied until he sees my head roll."

"No," Lady Li said, trying to comfort her. "I have known him for a long time, and I have only ever seen him try to get to the truth of the matter."

"But I'm telling the truth!" Wangshu said. "Why would he want me arrested when it was an accident?"

Lady Li sighed. "I am sure he feels that he is in a difficult position," she said. "After all, we did see the actual crime take place. I cannot think of another time when the person who committed a murder was not an actual murderer."

"So, I'm the first woman to perform opera in public," Wangshu said, holding her head high. "And I'm the first innocent murderer."

Lady Li had been so focused on saving Wangshu, she hadn't given much thought to the actual crime yet, but Wangshu's words resonated with her.

"Do you think that your performance might have something to do with the murder?" she asked.

"Of course, it does," Wangshu said. "You should see the stacks of angry letters in my dressing room."

"Wait here," Lady Li said and then walked over to the prince and Inspector Gong.

"...she's going to be furious," the prince was saying as she approached.

"Who is?" she interrupted.

"The empress," the prince said in annoyance. "Surely you know how important this was to her."

Lady Li shook her head. "I know she loves opera and was very proud of Wangshu, but she didn't speak to me about this."

"This was supposed to be her first big act to improve social attitudes toward women and people of lower classes," he explained. "You must understand how radical this whole experiment was."

"I do," Lady Li said. "In fact, I think that might have something to do with why Fanhua was killed. Wangshu said she has received many threatening letters. Whoever did this was probably furious about a woman taking the stage."

"I'll look into it," Inspector Gong said. "But I'm shocked that neither of you will let me arrest her. She's still a murderer."

"How can you be so rigid?" Lady Li asked, exasperated. "If you were riding a horse and...and..." She looked around for inspiration, her eyes falling on the bright red beard one of the actors was still wearing. "And the King of Hell jumped out from behind a tree, *intentionally* spooking the horse, and the wild horse trampled a person to death, who would be responsible? You for riding it or the King of Hell for causing the horse to run? Would it be fair for you to be put to death when the accident was not your fault?"

Inspector Gong pressed his lips and breathed out his nose, unwilling to admit that Lady Li had made a good point.

"If we wait to arrest her until we know the whole story," the prince said, "I might be able to persuade the ministry to act leniently with Wangshu. But if we arrest her now, the only evidence they will have is that she killed the man. I won't be able to protect her."

"Exactly," Lady Li said. She turned to the inspector and gently touched his arm, giving him a small smile for good measure. "I appreciate your dedication to justice. But arresting her now will only result in the death of another innocent person. It would be better to wait until you have the full story before presenting the case to the Ministry of Justice."

Inspector Gong threw up his arms. "Fine, you both win," he said, and Lady Li did her best to suppress her face from glowing in victory.

Some of the prince's guards returned with a sheet and laid it over the dead body.

"The audience was shockingly oblivious to what they witnessed tonight," the prince mused. "Perhaps keeping the death quiet for a while will help with tracking down the killer."

Inspector Gong nodded. "It won't stay a secret for long," he said. "These things never do."

"Then work quickly, inspector," the prince said, slapping his friend on the shoulder. "I'm going home. Keep me updated."

"Yes, your highness," the inspector grumbled.

"Is there any way I can assist you?" Lady Li asked the inspector sweetly.

"No," he said. "You should go home as well. I will be here all night interviewing the rest of the actors and the backstage crew."

"If you do need anything," she said, reaching out and squeezing his hand, "do let me know."

"Anything?" he asked quietly.

"Almost anything," she whispered back.

6

Inspector Gong watched as Lady Li walked away, swaying on her pot-bottom shoes. He didn't recall Swan having such desirable curves, but he had never really looked at her that closely before. He shook his head to clear his thoughts of both women so he could focus on finding out who would want an opera performer dead.

He walked over and pulled back the sheet from Fanhua's body to get a closer look. It was hard to see his face clearly through all the makeup, but he seemed to be fairly young. The costume was bulky, but he thought the man had a rather lithe build from what he remembered of the show. He motioned to one of the guards who had been ordered to stay behind to help him turn the body over. Fanhua's eyes were shut, but his jaw was clenched tightly. He'd been in considerable pain when he died, which was to be expected for being run through with a sword. Inspector Gong had, of course, never been mortally wounded in battle himself, but he had his share of scars from his years in the military and had seen firsthand the damage a blade could do to the human body.

He examined the wound as best as he could without actually removing the clothes. The costume was designed to look like military armor, but it was little more than several layers of fabric. Still, it would take some effort to make sure the sword went through the clothes and then deep enough into the body to kill the man. He found it hard to believe that Wangshu had no idea that something was wrong before it was too late.

He covered the body back up and then explained to one of the guards how to deliver the body to Dr. Xue, the only doctor Inspector Gong trusted with bodies in his cases. He didn't think Dr. Xue would be able to tell him anything he didn't already know, but the man often surprised him.

He looked up and noticed that Wangshu—and her guard—was gone. His heart sped up for a moment. He wouldn't blame her for running. Even though the prince had put a guard on her, it wouldn't be impossible for her to slip away. He had threatened to arrest her more than once. Her life was on the line. She would certainly run if she had the chance.

Several men and women who were not actors but worked with the troop and for the theater were clearing the stage and cleaning up.

"Where did Wangshu go?" the inspector asked no one in particular.

"She is in her dressing room," one of the women replied, pointing down a hallway.

Inspector Gong nodded his appreciation and went that way. He wasn't sure which room would be hers, but about halfway down he saw the prince's guard standing by an open door. The inspector nodded to him as he entered the room without knocking.

Wangshu had removed most of her costume and her

large headdress. She was sitting in front of a mirror at a dressing table removing more of her makeup with some moist towels. It was late, so the room was dim except for two candles on the dressing table and a few more scattered around the room. The room was small and crowded with costumes, props, and stacks of trunks with items spilling out of them. An uneaten bowl of noodles that had long gone cold sat on one end of a small, uncomfortable-looking couch.

Wangshu looked up at the inspector's reflection in her mirror but didn't respond as she went back to cleaning her face.

"This room is rather a disaster," he said as he ran his finger over the silk of one of the gowns hanging by the door.

"I haven't had time to unpack properly," Wangshu said. "I only arrived a few days ago and have no idea how long I'm staying."

"Why was that?" the inspector asked as he casually watched Wangshu for any clues in her demeanor.

"Fanhua was the troop's dan before I came along," Wangshu said. "And he was quite popular. I'm sure the troupe would like to see me gone as soon as possible so their lives can get back to normal. I wouldn't mind getting out of this hellhole myself."

Inspector Gong nodded. Fanhua had traditionally played the role of the young woman. That would explain why he didn't seem to have the build of a typical wusheng, a male character of military power.

"And how did Fanhua feel about being replaced?" he asked.

Wangshu froze, except for her eyes, which raised and stared at the inspector pointedly. Finally, she sighed, put her washcloth down, and turned in her chair to face him.

"Anything I say is going to make me look more guilty in your eyes."

The inspector looked around the room and spotted a stool under a pile of clothes. He pushed the clothes off and moved the stool closer to Wangshu so he could sit near her.

"Then you might as well tell me everything," he said. "It would be better for me to hear of any troubles between you and Fanhua from you than someone else."

Wangshu pressed her lips and looked away for a moment. She knew he was right; he only had to wait for her to come to terms with that face.

"Fanhua hated playing the wusheng," she said. "You saw how poorly he performed tonight. He wasn't mean to be a sheng, of any rank. He was born to play the dan."

"So how did you come to join this troop?" the inspector asked. "Aren't most troops families?"

"The Dashu Opera Troupe is the most popular in all of Peking," Wangshu said. "When the empress decided to make an example of me, she had to put me in the group that would have the largest audience. She couldn't have me perform with any back-alley group."

"So the empress ordered the troupe to take you on as a member," the inspector said. "How did the rest of the troupe feel about it?"

"You'd have to ask them," Wangshu said. "But the empress paid them handsomely for the honor, so I don't think the rest of them minded much."

"Who is the head of the troupe?" the inspector asked.

"Changpu," Wangshu said. "He played the Lord of Hell. His dressing room is at the end of the hall."

The inspector nodded, taking a mental note. "I'll speak to him later. So what was supposed to happen now? If Fanhua hadn't died, would you be going back to the

Forbidden City now that you've opened the door for other women?"

"That is what the empress told me," Wangshu said. "Well, she wanted me to perform here for a few weeks. Long enough for people to grow comfortable with the idea of a female dan. Then I could return to my own troop at the Forbidden City."

"So this was only a temporary arrangement?" the inspector asked. Wangshu nodded. It made no sense, then, for Wangshu to kill her rival when she wasn't planning to stay.

"At least, I hoped it was," Wangshu finally added. "But you know the empress. Her mind is changeable. If she liked the public's response toward me, she might have ordered me to stay longer."

"Do you think she would have ordered you to join the troop permanently?" he asked.

"I don't think so," Wangshu said. "I am the best dan the opera world has ever seen. And the empress always collects the best of everything for herself. She wouldn't want to let me go forever. But after I cleared the path, she might have ordered another woman to take my place."

Inspector Gong couldn't suppress a smile from the side of his mouth. While the character of Xueyan was a model of humility, Wangshu clearly had none. He had to admit, she was good, but he hadn't seen enough operas in his life to know if she was really the best.

"I'm going to ask you a hard question," the inspector said, leaning forward with his arms on his knees. "And it would be best if you answer truthfully. Will anyone else tell me that you had a reason to kill Fanhua?"

Wangshu cocked her head and blinked slowly. She leaned back in her seat. In truth, Inspector Gong couldn't yet see a reason why Wangshu would kill Fanhua. He was hoping that her reaction to this question would tell him something new. Most people would simply blurt out no, whether they were guilty or not. Some people would hesitate, as though really considering the question from other perspectives, but they would be anxious to say no. Wangshu's long, easy deliberation confused him. He wasn't sure what to make of it. Though the more he considered her, the less sure he was of her answers. After all, she—by her own account—was an incredible actress. Could he believe anything she said?

"No," she finally said. "I had no reason to kill Fanhua. If anything, he had reason to kill *me*. I was the one who took his place, after all."

"Do you think he hated you enough to want you dead?" the inspector asked. "Did you kill him preemptively? A form of self-defense?"

Wangshu laughed. "You are really grasping at straws now, inspector."

He reached a hand behind his neck and stretched. Perhaps he was. But it was late, or possibly early. He wasn't sure at this point. And he still had more interviews to do before people started forgetting what they saw.

He stood up to take his leave. "Where are you staying?" he asked.

Wangshu motioned toward the small, had couch. "Many of the actors live here at the theater, including me, for the time being."

"Then don't go anywhere," the inspector ordered. "I need to be able to locate you at all times."

Wangshu sighed with annoyance and turned away to finish cleaning up.

As the inspector left the room, he noticed that the

prince's guard's head was drooping. He slapped the guard on the arm to get his attention.

"Hey!" he said. "Don't let her out of your sight, do you understand?"

"Yes, sir!" the man said, standing to attention. "Of course, sir."

"I'd hate to see your head roll if she escapes," the inspector said as he walked down the hall toward the dressing room for the Lord of Hell.

The door was closed, but he could hear someone inside, so he knocked. "Changpu?" he said, recalling what Wangshu had said his name was.

A man he didn't recognize opened the door. "Yes?" the man asked.

"Changpu?" the inspector asked, confused.

"Yes," the man, who was now shorter, bald, and of average build, said. Stage makeup was truly magic. "Can I help you?"

Inspector Gong pushed his way into the room. "I need to ask you a few questions before I leave tonight."

The man sighed. "Very well. I was afraid this was coming but had hoped it could wait until tomorrow. I'm exhausted."

"I know the feeling," the inspector said. "I'll make this visit brief, but I'm sure we will be speaking a lot over the next few days."

"Then let's get to it," Changpu said as he motioned to a plush chair in the western style. Changpu took a seat for himself on a long couch. Wangshu's room was merely a closet compared to this. "I'm afraid I don't have anything to offer you in the way of refreshments."

"No need," the inspector said. "Wangshu said you are the leader of the troupe?"

"Yes," Changpu said with a smile, giving off an air of pride. "The Dashu troupe was founded over a hundred years ago by my great-grandfather down in Anhui. My grandfather moved us here before I was born."

"What prompted the move?" the inspector asked, not really caring about the history of the troupe, but he had found that getting people to talk about themselves was a good way to loosen them up for more probing questions later.

"The Manchu have always been great supporters of opera," Changpu said. "We were one of four troupes brought to Peking for the eightieth birthday of the great Qianlong Emperor. The current empress is also a great patron. She has elevated us from merely an entertainment for the masses to a respected art form."

The inspector nodded. Even he had noticed opera's growing popularity over the last few years.

"Most opera troupes are families," the Inspector said. "Was Fanhua related to you?"

"He was," Changpu said with a solemn nod. "My sister's son. But she died several years ago, and his father abandoned us to seek his fortune on Gold Mountain."

"Did he find it?" the inspector asked.

"We never heard from him again," Changpu said. "Whether he died on the journey over or is now a fat, rich lord, we have no idea."

"You don't seem particularly distraught over the death of your nephew," the inspector observed.

"What can I say to that?" Changpu asked, holding up his palms. "I have three children of my own and a business to run. I cared for the boy, of course, but I'm more concerned about what this will mean for ticket sales. He was quite popular with the ladies."

"But didn't he usually play the role of a woman?" the inspector asked.

Changpu laughed. "Who can understand the mind of a woman? Especially young, flighty girls like the ones he usually portrayed."

Inspector Gong filed that information away in the back of his mind to ponder over later. "So how did you feel about Wangshu being forced into the troupe and acting on stage?" he asked. "Some might take offense at having to replace a male actor with a lowly woman."

"Oh, I didn't care overmuch," Changpu said, and Inspector Gong couldn't help but raise a skeptic eyebrow. "It's true!" Changpu insisted. "You must understand, Peking Opera is a relatively new form of opera. Remember, we are from Anhui. We used to perform Huiju-style opera. And my wife, she is from a troupe from Hubei. They practically speak a different language. Peking Opera is always growing and changing. We constantly write new plays and new melodies. We are never afraid of trying something new and taking risks. Women are involved in every aspect of the opera already. My eldest daughter is a brilliant choreographer while my youngest daughter can write the sweetest love songs. She wrote the duet between the general and Xueyan you heard tonight. Were you not moved to tears by it?"

The inspector hadn't been, but he had noticed that several other people were.

"Letting a woman perform on stage was...inevitable," Changpu went on. "I know some smaller family troupes who don't have enough men sometimes allow their daughters to perform. They don't advertise it and most people can't tell under the makeup and costumes. And the fat price the empress paid to give Wangshu the chance to perform? Well, that was a welcome incentive."

Inspector Gong felt a twitch behind his eye. This wasn't getting him anywhere. No one seemed to have a reason to kill anyone.

"Why would Wangshu kill Fanhua?" the inspector asked.

"No idea," Changpu said, flabbergasted. "If I hadn't seen it, I wouldn't have believed it. Fanhua was the person who had been wronged, not Wangshu. Fanhua hated playing the wusheng, and he wasn't right for it. But I didn't have any other roles for him to play."

"But the situation was only temporary," the inspector said. "Wangshu wouldn't be here forever."

"Well, I don't know about that," Changpu said. "Depending on how things went, I might have tried to persuade her to stay, or I could have hired a new woman if she left if the patrons grew to prefer a female dan. Opera is nothing if not adaptable. It would depend on the audience and whether they preferred a man or woman in the role."

The inspector nodded and added Changpu to his list of suspects. The man had no love of his nephew and was probably going to replace him on a permanent basis. If he had no role for him to play, he would just bring the whole production down. He could have killed him to get rid of him. Though it seemed like a rather dramatic solution to the problem.

Inspector Gong stood and felt a little lightheaded. "I think that is enough for tonight," he said. "It has been a long evening."

"Too long," Changpu said as he motioned toward the door.

"Do you live here at the theater?" Inspector Gong asked.

Changpu laughed. "Certainly not. I have a house in the Xiyuan District."

Inspector Gong nodded. He knew the area. It was where many wealthy Han Chinese lived. His troupe certainly had prospered if he lived there.

"Wangshu said many of the troupe members are living here at the theater," the inspector said.

"Some do, if they have nowhere else to go," Changpu said as he followed the inspector out of the room and locked the door behind him with a key from a large ring.

"Do you have a key to Fanhua's room?" the inspector asked. "I need to have a look at it and make sure no one goes in there until the investigation is over."

"Of course," Changpu said, removing a key from the ring.

"Which one was his?" the inspector asked.

"First room," Changpu said, pointing back down the hallway past Wangshu's room.

"Thanks," the inspector said. "I hope you have a restful night."

"I doubt it," Changpu said. "But I appreciate the sentiment."

The inspector walked down the hall toward Fanhua's room, but he watched Changpu leave. He wasn't sure how seriously he should consider Changpu a suspect, but it was a possibility. He had a motive, however small and unreasonable it seemed to the inspector. After all, he had seen people kill for much less. He would have one of his own men follow Changpu and keep an eye on his residence to make sure he didn't flee in the night.

When he got to Fanhua's room, he was surprised to find the door unlocked. He cursed himself. He should have made sure the room was secure immediately. He gasped when he entered the room.

It looked as though it had been ransacked. The clothing racks had been toppled, trunks knocked over, and furniture upturned. He had no idea if anything had been stolen, but the room was so crowded with expensive costumes, he rather thought not. As he stepped through the room to the dressing table, the smashed mirror confirmed his suspicions.

This was an act of rage.

7

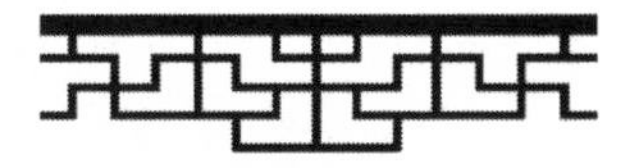

The theater had long been empty by the time Lady Li left, so she was surprised to see so many people still milling about outside. As she exited, many excited young women rushed toward the open door, nearly pushing Lady Li back inside. When they saw it was Lady Li who was exiting, they all seemed to groan with disappointment in unison.

Lady Li chuckled in confusion as she made her way through the crowd. "What is going on?" she asked a young woman at random. All of the women appeared to be rather young, only in their teens. And most of them appeared to be upper-class, judging by their clothes. The women were both Manchu and Han, which Lady Li could tell by whether or not they had bound feet.

"We were hoping you were Fanhua," the girl replied.

"The actor who played the wusheng?" Lady Li asked.

"Humph," the girl scoffed. "For tonight. He's usually the dan."

"The best dan," another young girl piped up. "The most beautiful, elegant dan in the world!"

"I wouldn't know," Lady Li said. "I never saw him before tonight." These young women were apparently very fond of Fanhua. Lady Li thought it best they didn't know just yet that their idol was dead since they didn't seem to know already. If these women spent a lot of time with Fanhua, or even just talking about him amongst each other, they might know something important about him or his lifestyle that could have led to his death. Lady Li decided to keep engaging them.

"Oh, you poor thing," another girl said. "Then you've never truly seen an opera!"

Lady Li couldn't help but laugh. "Surely I have."

"It's no matter," a haughty young woman with her arms crossed replied. "I'm sure that dreadful Wangshu won't last long. She can't hold a lantern to Fanhua!"

"But isn't it more authentic for a woman to play a woman?" Lady Li asked, hoping to get a strong reaction from the women. And she was not disappointed. They all seemed to gasp in horror at once.

"It's improper!" one woman said.

"Immoral!" cried another.

"It's obscene!" said another. "She should be ashamed to flaunt herself in public like that!"

"Women should not take part in public affairs," another said, quoting the familiar admonition from Confucius that made Lady Li grimace.

"What made Fanhua better?" Lady Li asked.

"He's so beautiful," one girl said wistfully, and several others murmured their agreements.

"He's so gentle," said another. "When I met him after a show last week, he reached out and touched my face so softly, I almost didn't feel it." She sighed at the memory.

"You have all met him?" Lady Li asked. "Are you his friends?"

The women giggled.

"Some of us are friends," the haughty young woman said. "Some of us are more than that."

Lady Li turned to her with a raised eyebrow of doubt. She couldn't believe a proper young lady like this girl would claim to be "more than friends" with an actor.

"And what's your name?" Lady Li asked her, though she almost didn't expect her to answer.

"Liu Baoah," the girl said, holding her chin high.

"And you were...*are* very close to Fanhua?" Lady Li asked.

"You could say that," Baoah said, trying to act nonchalant about it.

"Baoah thinks she's Fanhua's favorite," another girl said playfully. "But really I am!"

"Shut up, Liling!" Baoah said with a push.

"No, it's me!" another girl said, then all the girls devolved into a fit of laughter.

Lady Li smiled at them but turned her attention back to Baoah.

"He is a frequent guest in my home," Baoah said. "My baba is a patron."

That made some sense. If her parents were fond of the opera, and even supported it financially, the girl would have more opportunities to associate with such a person. Still, she doubted her parents knew about or approved of her standing around outside a theater at three in the morning.

"I'm thinking of becoming a patron myself," Lady Li said. "I'd love to talk to you and your parents about it."

"Mama and Baba love to talk about the opera," Baoah said. "We live on Chundu Road, the Liu family compound."

"I'll make it a point to call on you soon," Lady Li said. She then turned to the girl Baoah called Liling. "And who are your parents?"

"The Chan family," she said, hiding her mouth behind her sleeve. "Also on Chundu."

"Perhaps we will meet again as well," Lady Li said. She then nodded to both of the girls, who gave her a small bow in return. She found her sedan chair waiting for her and climbed inside.

As soon as she sat down, all the excitement from the evening seemed to rush out of her. The night was turning into early morning, and Lady Li knew she would have very little time to sleep before the next day began. Even though she didn't have to be up before breakfast, she was a light sleeper and was usually awake as soon as the servants started their chores around the house with the first cock crow.

When she arrived home, all she wanted to do was slink into her room and fall into bed, but she was dismayed to find many of the lanterns still lit and the servants rushing about nervously.

As she crossed the courtyard, Eunuch Bai approached her with his head down.

"What's going on?" she asked. "Are the girls all right?"

"They are fine, my lady," he said. "They went right to bed. But there is another matter..."

"What is it?" she asked. "Out with it. I'm exhausted."

"It's Lady Swan," he was all he said. He didn't need to say more. Lady Li felt the fury rush to her cheeks. She kicked off her pot-bottom shoes as hard as she could into a wall to get some of her anger out before she confronted Swan.

"You should breathe, my lady," Eunuch Bai said.

Normally, it would be out of place for a servant to counsel his mistress, but he knew that she had been ashamed of her anger toward Swan's opium addiction in the past and would not want a repeat of such actions.

She took a deep breath and counted to five before going to Swan's room. The scene was as she suspected it would be. Swan was slumped in a chair while two maids were holding her upright and trying to get her to drink some weak tea. Two other maids who had been watching quickly vanished when Lady Li entered the room.

"What happened?" Lady Li demanded. "How did she get it?"

"I found one of the floorboards disturbed," Eunuch Bai said. "There was a substantial amount of opium hidden there. She must have been stockpiling it for weeks knowing you would contain her to the house eventually."

Lady Li rubbed her forehead. "I don't understand," she mumbled. "She said she wanted to marry Inspector Gong. Doesn't she know that this could ruin everything? If his mother finds out she eats opium before the wedding, she will call it off, no matter the shame it might bring to the family. Calling off a betrothal would be better than having an opium-eating daughter-in-law."

"When it comes to the allure of the clouds," Eunuch Bai said, "I don't think an addict pays heed to such reason."

Lady Li watched Swan's bobbing head, her eyes closed, her skin clammy. She was completely unresponsive to the maids trying to help her wake up.

"How much did she have?" Lady Li asked.

"A lot," Eunuch Bai said. "She apparently dismissed her maids early for the night, saying she was tired. I went to check on her after I put the girls to bed. She had most likely been smoking for hours. I found her on the floor. I think she slid off the bed at some point and didn't notice. Thankfully the pipe had long gone out."

Lady Li squeezed her eyes shut at the thought of Swan burning their house down in an opium stupor.

"She's not going to wake up anytime soon," Lady Li told the maids. "Put her in one of the guest bedrooms. Who knows how much more opium she might have hidden within her own walls. Or within her kang or in her closet. And she must have a maid watcher her at all times. She is no longer allowed to dismiss them on her own."

One of the maids bowed and then scurried off to prepare one of the other rooms.

"All the opium you found," Lady Li said to Eunuch Bai, "take it out of the house and burn it. Then pull up all the floorboards in here, rip open her kang, pull down every wall hanging. If she has hidden any more opium in here, I want it found."

"Yes, my lady," Eunuch Bai said. He then opened his mouth to say more, but then he stopped.

"What?" Lady Li asked, exasperated. "Just out with it."

"I have heard that when an opium addict is suddenly cut off from the drug," he said, "the addiction can get worse. The person can get very ill, possibly die."

"I don't understand," Lady Li said. "Can't the drug kill her?"

"Yes," he said. "I am not an expert on this, but it is as if her body has learned to live with it. It thinks it is a necessary part of life. If the body suddenly doesn't have it, it simply cannot function."

"That's mad," Lady Li said, unable to believe what she was hearing. "Are you saying we should keep giving her opium? Look at her!"

"I'm not saying we ignore her addiction," Eunuch Bai

said with a clarity and calm Lady Li wished she could emulate. "But that we need help. We cannot cure her on our own. She needs a doctor."

"What can a doctor do?" Lady Li asked. "She's not sick, just stupid."

"But she has made her body sick," Eunuch Bai explained. "Acupuncture, medicines, there are things a doctor could do to help her recover safely."

"I can't send for my doctor," Lady Li said. "Then he'd...*know*. He could tell someone. He could warn Gong Furen." Her personal physician was considered one of the best in the city, but she wasn't sure she could trust him with such a sensitive subject.

"We need to find someone discreet," Eunuch Bai said. "Someone we can trust."

Lady Li rubbed her forehead again as she paced. She was so exhausted she couldn't think straight.

"I don't know anyone like that," she said. "I don't deal with those kinds of people."

"But you know someone who does," Eunuch Bai said. Lady Li cocked her head at him and frowned. He chuckled. "Unfortunately, I'm not speaking of myself this time."

"You mean Inspector Gong?" Lady Li asked.

"He already knows about Lady Swan's addiction and has agreed to marry her anyway," he reasoned. "He surely knows someone who could treat her and be discreet about it."

"I suppose," Lady Li said. "She will be his responsibility soon enough anyway."

"Exactly," Eunuch Bai said.

"The room is ready, my lady," one of the maids said upon her return.

Lady Li nodded. "Thank you." She then went to Swan's

side and motioned for Eunuch Bai to help her. They each draped one of Swan's arms over their shoulders and slowly moved her to the other room. She wasn't heavy. Gong Furen had noted how thin Swan was, and Lady Li had to admit that she wasn't just a skinny woman—she was barely more than bones. Hopefully she would eat more food once she was completely cut off from her opium supply.

When they got to the other room, they laid Swan in the bed. It wasn't cold, but Swan's skin felt cool and clammy to the touch. Lady Li put a blanket over her and ordered a brazier to be brought in and lit.

"You should go to bed now, my lady," Eunuch Bai said. "One of the maids can stay up with her."

Lady Li ran her hand over Swan's brow and could almost feel the pain the girl was in. She felt a sudden pang of guilt over leaving her at home this evening. She hadn't really left her behind out of decency to protect Swan's reputation. She'd done it out of spite. And look what happened. She could have died from ingesting so much opium.

"No," Lady Li said. "I'll stay with her. She needs someone who won't fall asleep and not be there for her if she needs anything."

"Then I will stay as well," Eunuch Bai said as he pulled over a chair and sat in it.

"There is no need for such gallantry," Lady Li chided. "Go to bed, you old fool."

Eunuch Bai laughed. "I'm younger than you."

With a sigh and roll of her eyes, she knew that there was nothing she could do to get Eunuch Bai to leave, so she simply accepted that she was going to have a visitor for the night. She took Swan's hand in her own and sat back to wait for the sunrise.

8

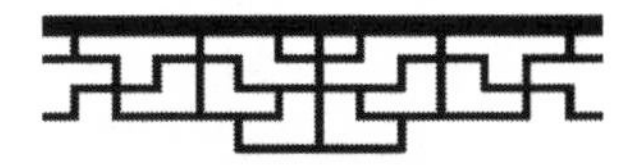

"Wake up, Anguo!" his mother shrieked as she threw open the curtain covering the window to his room, letting the sun in and shine directly on his face.

Inspector Gong groaned and turned away. If the sun was shining that brightly, he knew he had overslept, but he had no idea how much sleep he had actually gotten that night. By the time he stumbled into bed, he heard the servants starting their morning tasks. He needed to get up, but he also needed to rest his mind if he was to be at his best.

"Go away, Ma," he moaned as he pulled a blanket over his face.

"Get up," she said as she pulled the covering back. "We need to talk about that girl."

He rolled onto his back and rubbed his eyes. "I can't talk about this," he said. "There was a murder at the opera last night..."

"There was a murder at the opera?" his mother exclaimed. Then he remembered that they were trying to keep that a secret for the time being while he tried to flush out the killer.

"Dammit," he said, sitting up and stretching. "You weren't supposed to know that. Don't tell anyone with your big mouth, understand?"

"I don't care anyway," his mother said as she walked around the room picking dirty clothes up off the floor and tossing them out the door for a maid to collect. "Bunch of low-class people, performing for money. Practically riverbed beggars is all they are. And now letting a woman perform? What is this world coming to?"

"Forget it," he said as he went to his washstand and poured some water into a bowl to splash his face with. "The point was that I can't worry about whatever you're in a huff about this time. I have to focus on this new case."

"Bah," his mother said with a wave of her arms. "There is always a new case. Someone dying. Someone stealing. Someone starting a fight. You can't keep putting off your life just because someone else made a bad decision."

He sighed and rolled his eyes in the mirror of his washing table. He needed to shave his chin. He was looking a bit scruffy. His queue was becoming a bit unkempt as well. He needed to brush his hair out, have it oiled and waxed and re-plaited. He was due for a head shave as well. He should ask one of the maids to do it for him, but he didn't know when he would have time. Even on a normal day he usually didn't get home until after most of the servants were asleep. And he rarely had normal days.

He cleared his throat and headed for the door. "Well, now that you've gotten me up, I might as well get to work."

"Don't you dare, Gong Anguo!" his mother called after him as they went to the large shared dining room where several of his siblings were having breakfast.

He sat at the table and a maid served him a steaming

bowl of congee with pickled vegetables on top and some steamed buns.

"We have to talk about Lady Swan," his mother said, pushing her older son out of the way so she could sit right next to Inspector Gong.

He ripped open a bun so the meat inside could cool. "What about her?" he asked, not really wanting to know. "Didn't you meet with Lady Li about her? Isn't this settled yet?"

"I met with Lady Li," his mother confirmed. "But nothing is settled yet. I wish you would reconsider."

"Why?" the inspector asked, dipping the bun into his congee. "What can you possibly have against her?"

His mother blew out her cheeks. "What *don't* I have against her? She's too old. She's used up. She's not one of us. Did you even ask the prince? What is the point in continuing until you have his permission?"

"I did speak with the prince," he said, not wanting to address his mother's other baseless concerns. "But we got distracted by the thing at the opera. I'll have to talk to him again later."

"What thing at the opera?" his sister Daiyu asked.

"Someone went and got murdered," his mother growled. "What else is new? We need to deal with Swan now."

"Who was murdered?" his brother Zhuang asked, bouncing his little girl on his lap.

"Dammit, Ma!" Inspector Gong snapped. "What did I say about your big mouth?"

"Oh, this must be good," his other sister Biyu said. "What happened?"

"Shut up, you yapping dogs," his mother yelled, slapping her hand on the table. "Look at me, Anguo. It makes no sense to marry this girl. Take her for a concubine, yes, but not a wife."

"I'm not married, Ma," Inspector Gong said. "If I don't take her as a wife, it will be a grave insult to her, and to Lady Li."

"But what about the insult to *me*?" his mother cried. "Have you no thought for the woman who carried you in her own body for months on end? Who nursed you for five long years?"

His siblings sputtered in laughter at that, and his face grew red. "Ma..." he warned.

"What have I ever done to deserve such treatment by my own son?" she lamented.

"You should have been an opera singer," Inspector Gong said. "You would put those supposed actors I saw last night to shame."

"Stop making such jokes!" his mother said, slapping his arm. "Please, consider your mother before you make this mistake."

"When I didn't want to marry, you said I was punishing you," he said, fed up. "Now, when I want to marry, you say she isn't good enough, even though she was good enough for a Manchu lord not long ago."

"You really want some Manchu—" She spit at the floor for good measure. "—bastard's castaway?"

"She's not a castaway," he said. "She's a widow. A woman worthy of respect. If anything, she is granting you a great honor in willing to humble herself as your daughter-in-law. If she remained a widow, her name would be carved on the temple gates and young wives would be forced to make offerings to her day and night. I'll not dishonor her by making her a concubine. And you will treat her kindly when she comes here. Am I clear?"

"Fine!" his mother said, standing up quickly. Too quickly on her bound feet. She squinted but showed no other sign of pain all the children knew she felt but were too polite to comment on. Daiyu and Biyu grimaced in sympathy. "But bring me the approval for marriage from Prince Kung. I'll scrape and bow to Lady Li no further until I know this marriage is even going to happen." She turned and walked with her back straight. She would have stomped had it been possible, but she slammed the sliding door shut behind her instead.

"That was poorly done, brother," Zhuang said as soon as their mother was gone but probably still within earshot. They all knew that her hearing her other children defend her would go a long way toward soothing her bruised ego. "She's not entirely wrong about this marriage raising eyebrows in the community."

"What would it even be like having a Manchu in the family?" Biyu wondered. "Will you have to bow to her every morning, brother? Will she let you bind your daughters' feet?"

He didn't respond because he hadn't actually thought about what it would be like marrying a woman from a different ethnic group.

"Mothers bind their daughters' feet," Daiyu said. "If Swan's feet aren't bound, she obviously won't bind her daughters' feet, even if her daughters are Han. She won't know how. She won't see the value in it."

"I hadn't even considered that," Biyu said, shaking her head. "No wonder Ma is so against this marriage."

"Can we talk about something else?" Inspector Gong asked, even though at this point he was only picking at his food, having lost his appetite. Why did everything have to be so complicated? He just wanted to wed and bed Swan so he could stop thinking about Lady Li all the time.

"Like murder?" Daiyu asked, leaning forward conspiratorially.

"Shit," Inspector Gong sighed, at this point simply dropping his spoon into his bowl. He had hoped she had forgotten about that. "No, I am not talking to you about the murder at the opera last night."

"Come on!" she begged, pulling on his sleeve. "Tell me! I was so sad I had to miss the show last night."

"What are you doing going to the opera?" Inspector Gong asked, raising his eyebrow. "Does Ma know about this?"

"She just looks the other way," Daiyu said. "It's harmless fun. And all the girls go. Fanhua is just so gorgeous. If our parents forbade us from going, we'd just sneak out."

"What are you talking about?" the inspector asked, confused. "What girls? And you think Fanhua is good looking? He looks like a girl."

"That's the appeal, apparently," Zhuang said as he helped his own little daughter hold her chopsticks. "According to my wife, young unmarried girls are drawn to effeminate men."

The inspector turned to Daiyu. "Is this true? Why?"

"I don't know," Daiyu said. "I'm not allowed to talk to any real boys, so Fanhua is just...safe, I guess."

Inspector Gong nodded. Unmarried girls were carefully guarded, rarely let out of the house for any reason other than attending temple or visiting the daughters of other noble families. Daiyu was only sixteen, and Biyu fifteen. They were of marriageable age, yet probably still too young to know what they would actually like in a man. Not that it mattered. If they wanted tall burley men or thin, scholarly ones, they wouldn't have a choice in who they married. He wondered if their mother had been making arrangements for them. It was strange he hadn't heard anything about a marriage for Daiyu at least.

"So who died?" Biyu asked. "Was it Wangshu? I heard that lots of Fanhua's admirers hate her."

"No, it wasn't Wangshu, surprisingly," the inspector said.

"So who was it?" Daiyu asked. "Tell me. Was it someone in the audience?"

The inspector paused for a moment. He hadn't planned on telling anyone, but Daiyu knew a surprising amount about the theater and Fanhua, more than he ever would have. Maybe she could tell him something about Fanhua's admirers that would be useful.

"It was Fanhua," he finally said. "Fanhua is dead."

Daiyu blinked. Then she sat back. "You...you're lying," she said. "You're teasing me because you know I like him. You're such a jerk!"

"I'm not lying, Daiyu," he said seriously. "Fanhua was killed last night."

He watched as all the color drained from her face and tears welled up in her eyes and then spilled down her cheeks. "No! No! This can't be true!"

Biyu patted her sister's back to comfort her. "Oh, Daiyu, I'm so sorry!"

"Good job, Anguo," Zhuang said as his daughter started fussing and he stood to take her from the room.

"What?" Inspector Gong asked. "What is happening here? Why are you so upset, Daiyu? He's just an actor."

"Just an actor?" Daiyu asked as she rubbed her eyes with her sleeves. "He's just the most beautiful actor. The sweetest, kindest, most gentle person."

"What the hell do you know about what kind of person

he is?" the inspector asked. "You shouldn't be getting so close to him. He might play a woman, but he's still a man. You should think about your reputation!"

"You're one to talk, Manchu lover!" she yelled as she stood and tottered out of the room on her bound feet, Biyu stumbling away behind her.

Inspector Gong ran his hands down his face. "What did I do to deserve this?" he asked the kitchen god over the doorway.

While his sister's reaction irked him—there was no way she should have had such an emotional reaction to a man she wasn't betrothed to—it did give him some insight into just how popular Fanhua was with young women. Would Daiyu's reaction ripple throughout the theater community? What was the relationship between Fanhua and the women? Did they think they were in love with him? Or that he was in love with them? Was he the sort of person who would lead a woman along?

He needed to look into this deeper. He also needed to return to the theater to learn more about the rest of the opera troupe.

He gathered his things and was about to leave the house when a servant approached with a note.

It was a summons from Lady Li, asking him to come to her mansion immediately. He cursed again. If Lady Li was sending for him, it could only be bad news.

9

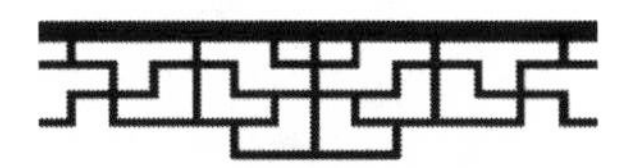

Lady Li gasped when she opened her eyes. She didn't mean to fall asleep. She couldn't have been out long. She turned to find Swan sleeping soundly, so she sighed in relief. She stood up and rubbed her neck and back. The chair had been a terrible place to try and rest.

Eunuch Bai walked in and handed her a cup of pu'er tea.

"You didn't bother trying to sleep at all, did you?" Lady Li asked as she took the cup and breathed in the earthy aroma as she walked to the door and looked out over the garden.

He stood next to her. "I don't think anyone did except for your daughters and mother-in-law."

"I am glad that Swan did not disturb Popo," Lady Li said, blowing on her tea. "She needs her rest."

"Popo's health has greatly improved since coming to live here," Eunuch Bai said. "Loneliness can be its own illness."

"At least I've been able to do right by one person," Lady Li said. She watched as the servants went about their business now that their mistress was awake. One person swept the walkways while another skimmed debris from the koi pond. Another servant entered the front gate with a brace of live ducks over his shoulder.

"You have done right by all your people," Eunuch Bai comforted. "You cannot blame yourself for Swan's misery and her poor way of coping. You did not make her a widow or introduce her to opium. Who could have known that things would turn out like this?"

Lady Li nodded. She knew he was right and there was no point in arguing. But as lady of the manor everything that happened within its walls was her responsibility, so she couldn't shake the feelings of guilt that settled upon her whenever she thought of Swan.

She sat on the edge of Swan's bed and wetted a cloth, which she wiped over Swan's brow.

"I want you to send for Inspector Gong," Lady Li said. "He will be preoccupied with the murder at the opera, but he must see to his domestic responsibilities as well."

Eunuch Bai tried not to laugh. "I am sure the thought of him suddenly having domestic responsibilities will come as a shock to him."

"Good," Lady Li said. "Let him learn what he is really getting into."

"I'll send him a note at once," he said.

"Wait a little while," Lady Li said. "It is still early. Let him rest a bit longer."

"And what about you, my lady?" Eunuch Bai asked. "As you can see, Swan is fine, for now. Why don't you lay down? I can fetch you if there is any change."

Lady Li was tired, exhausted actually, but her mind was alert. Now that she didn't need to worry about Swan, her thoughts returned to the murder of Fanhua and the strange girls she met outside the theater.

"No," she said. "There is something I need to do."

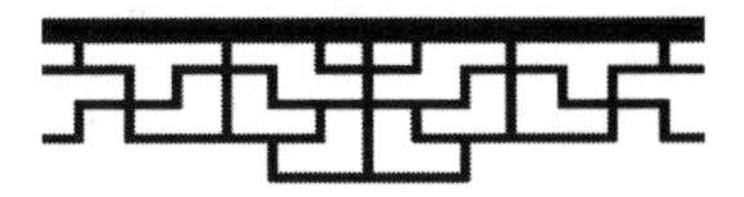

Even though it was early, it was not too early to make a social call. Women were often expected to wake with the first light and begin the business of running their household, though Lady Li doubted much was required of Baoah if she was able to sneak off in the evenings to attend opera performances.

She rode in her sedan chair to the Liu family compound. Lady Li's home was a mansion, but it was still rather on the small side compared to the home she now stood in front of.

In Chinese families, first sons were not the only beneficiaries of an inheritance. All sons usually divided a family's assets upon the death of a patriarch—and that included the family home. But since a home could not be cut up and moved, most sons never left their family home, but instead stayed there along with their wives and children, and eventually their grandsons and their families. If a family had land, the home could be expanded to accommodate the growing family, with more buildings and rooms added on as needed, but they would still get crowded. Usually it would take a break in the family relationship—a sibling rivalry between brothers or a competition between sisters-in-law too great to overcome—that would result in some members of the family finally moving out and establishing their own residences. From the looks of things, the Liu family had not had any disruptions for a very long time. The main wall was a whole block long, and the many layers of roofs could be seen even from the street level as the house encroached on and then took over the hill behind it.

As Lady Li knocked on the door and waited for someone to answer, she thought about just how small her family was in comparison—and how it would be even smaller as soon as Swan left her. While she treasured her solitude most of the time, she did often miss the loud, happy home she grew up in, with many brothers, mothers, and aunts surrounding her. She wondered if her own daughters were missing something in their life by growing up so isolated.

A male servant answered the door, and Lady Li explained that she was a friend of Baoah. He let her inside, and she followed him down long passageways, up a stone incline, and past several large doors before finally knocking on one.

"Baobao," the man called. "You have a guest."

Lady Li heard some rather unladylike cursing from inside the room as Baoah stumbled toward the door. The door squeaked open, and Baoah squinted in the daylight that dared to shine upon her unwashed face.

"What?" Baoah mumbled. "Who is it?"

"We met last night," Lady Li said. "At the opera. Do you remember?"

"Huh? Oh, right," Baoah said, backing up and opening the door a little wider. "Sure, come in. What do you want?"

Lady Li cocked an eyebrow at the servant, who shook

his head in shame as he walked away, and entered the room.

"I hope you will forgive the early call," she said.

Baoah went over to the other side of the room and pulled some drapes back from a large latticed window to let some more light in. She then moved a kettle over a fireplace.

"It's nothing," Baoah said.

"I just couldn't sleep after the performance last night," Lady Li said. "It was just so exciting. Especially Fanhua. I was hoping you could tell me more about him. Maybe tell me how I could meet him."

"Meet him?" Baoah said, her eyes wide as if she were suddenly wide awake.

"Yes," Lady Li said innocently. "You said you were his friend. I thought you might be able to arrange something."

"Oh, right," Baoah said. "Well, everything is up in the air right now, you know. I'm not sure what's going on."

"What do you mean?" Lady Li asked, playing dumb. She took a seat on a bench near the fireplace.

"With Wangshu playing his role," Baoah said. "I have his schedule here." She rummaged through a stack of papers on a nearby table that looked like performance programs.

Lady Li stepped over to have a look and found the program from the performance last night along with several other programs, some dating from years ago.

"Careful with those," Baoah said, taking them from Lady Li and carefully putting them back in a pile. "Some of those are nearly falling apart."

"You see a lot of operas," Lady Li remarked. "You must have such an appreciation for the art."

Baoah handed a paper with performance names and times on it. "Not really," she said. "I just love Fanhua. I've seen every show he's ever been in. That was his schedule for the month when he was still playing the dan, but now, who knows when he'll be performing, or what part he'll even be playing." She removed the kettle from the fireplace and poured the hot water into two cups that were sitting nearby. She then sprinkled some tea leaves into the cups and handed one to Lady Li.

Lady Li took the cup and had a small sip even though she wondered how long it had been since the cup had been cleaned. She turned around, taking in the messy room. She saw an opera mask hanging on the wall.

"That's an interesting piece," Lady Li said.

"Yeah," Baoah said. "Most opera performers don't wear masks anymore. They just paint their faces. But Fanhua wore that in *Peach Tree Dreams*. He was brilliant in it. But he always is."

"And he gave you the mask?" Lady Li asked. "That was quite generous of him."

"He might not have seen me slip it into my sleeve," Baoah said with a naughty smile.

Lady Li made a face like she was shocked—which she was—then she laughed, hoping to make Baoah think she approved of her petty theft, which might not have been so petty considering how expensive opera costume pieces could be.

"I have quite a few pieces I've pinched from him over the years," Baoah said. She opened a drawer and pulled out a few treasures. "This is a handkerchief he used when he played Madam Butterfly. This is a fan he carried as one of the daughters in *Blue Eyes, Blue Sorrow*. And this is my pride and joy." She walked over and pulled a long lance out from behind her kang. "He used this in *The Generals of the Yang Family*."

Lady Li felt a lump in her throat at seeing the weapon in the girl's hand, even though she knew the murder weapon had been a sword. "How...how did you steal that without Fanhua knowing," Lady Li finally managed to ask.

"That's my little secret," Baoah said before putting it back in its hiding place.

"Well, how about telling me why you would steal his things at all?" Lady Li asked.

Baoah cocked her head to the side like it was no big deal. "I don't know. All of us, his admirers, we all collect little things he's used and touched. Helps feel close to him I guess."

"I see," Lady Li said. "Like a lock of hair from a lover."

"Exactly," Baoah said. "You wouldn't happen to have a lock of his hair, would you?"

"Thankfully no," Lady Li said. "You don't think anyone would hurt poor Fanhua trying to get a piece of him, do you?"

"What?" Baoah asked with an awkward giggle. "Hurt him? We love him and only want to protect him."

"Of course," Lady Li said. "Do you follow any other opera performers? The Lord of Hell, perhaps?"

"That old goat?" Baoah sputtered a laugh. "That whole troupe only has an audience because of Fanhua. There is no one else at that theater worth seeing."

"There must be other performers out there worthy of admiration," Lady Li prodded. "Since we don't know Fanhua's schedule, who else should I go see?"

"The only other person with nearly as large a following would be Huangjian," Baoah said. "He is with the Xishan Szechuan group. He's a face changer."

Lady Li nodded. She had seen face changing opera

before, but it had been a while. It was quite fascinating to watch.

"Do you have some of his stolen items around here too?" Lady Li asked conspiratorially.

"No, I don't follow him myself," Baoah said. "He plays a man. What's beautiful about that?"

"What's wrong with him playing a man?" Lady Li asked. "He is one, just like Fanhua."

"But he doesn't understand us," Baoah said. "He doesn't know what we go through, how we are treated. How our feet hurt and the pain we feel at being ripped from our families."

Lady Li nodded as she began to understand. Baoah wasn't in love with Fanhua because he dressed like a woman, but because she believed he was the only man who could understand what it was like to be a woman. That was just another illusion, though.

Lady Li wondered if Fanhua was just as good of an actor off stage as on it. After all, he didn't really know what it was to be a woman. He only played a part, and at the end of the day he could take off his shoes and remove his face paint and return to the world of men. But he had been able to convince his admirers that he truly understood them. That he practically was one of them. They trusted him because of that. They loved him.

Had he betrayed that trust, that love? Had one of his admirers killed him because of it?

Lady Li had no idea, and she wouldn't know where to start finding out. Who knew how many followers like Baoah Fanhua had.

Lady Li stood to leave. "Well, I'm sure I have taken up enough of your morning. I should be going. But if you find out when Fanhua is performing again, do let me know." She wondered if it was cruel of her to continue letting the girl think the object of her obsession was still alive, but she couldn't bring herself to tell her that Fanhua was really dead.

Lady Li decided to take her leave. "Thank you for receiving me this morning," she said with a polite nod of her head. "I hope to see you at another performance again soon."

As she climbed back into her sedan chair, exhaustion once again climbed over her. The excitement of calling on Baoah wore off, and she was beginning to regret that she had sent for Inspector Gong. She only wanted to return home and rest.

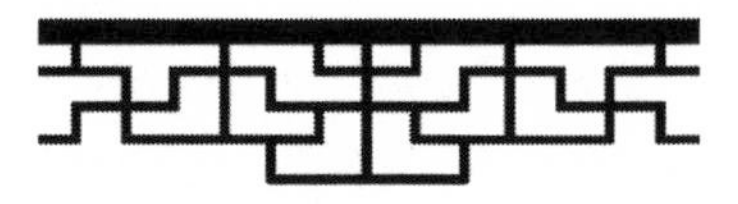

"What have you done?" she yelled at her girls as soon as she entered the gate.

The girls had both gotten into her closet and pulled out some of her nicest robes. They had put on batou head-dresses and seemed to have attached every piece of jewelry she owned to them. They had also painted each other's faces with bright red lips and blue eyes and white cheeks with makeup from Lady Li's dressing table. They were running around, chasing each other with sticks and singing the songs from the opera they had heard the night before.

"I'm an opera singer!" Second Daughter triumphantly yelled, waving her stick in the air.

"But you are running my clothes and losing my jewels!" Lady Li snapped as she gripped both her daughters by the arms and led them back toward the living quarters. "Where is your nursemaid? Or Eunuch Bai? Or Popo?" she asked.

But she soon found out. Swan had awoken and was hunched over a chamber pot dry heaving since she had nothing in her stomach to evacuate. She was also feverish yet freezing, trying to pull a blanket over her shoulders as she leaned over the bowl. The whole of the household staff appeared to be trying either to comfort Swan or fighting over the best course of treatment for her. Popo thought Swan should be given a warm bath while a maid thought she needed some medicinal tea. The cook was trying to figure out who needed breakfast while Eunuch Bai was trying to clean up the mess Swan must have made when she had woken up.

"Quiet!" Lady Li yelled over the cacophony, and everyone silenced save Swan's simpering. "Popo, please take the girls. Clean them up and serve them breakfast. Lingling, go to the yard and find any jewels the girls may have lost before the chickens eat them, then see if you can salvage my robes the girls are wearing. Xiaoting, clean this room. I will see to Swan. Eunuch Bai, please see to anything else I have missed."

"Yes, mistress," everyone said in unison with a bow.

It didn't matter how tired she was, her job was never done. She grabbed a basin of warm water and a cloth and kneeled by Swan's side. She brushed Swan's hair aside and washed her face with the cloth.

"What...what is happening to me?" Swan cried.

"Don't you remember?" Lady Li asked.

"I never remember," Swan said. "That's the whole point. I know I shouldn't keep taking the opium, but for some reason, I do. And when I wake up, I don't remember why I did it. How did I talk myself into it? How can I stop myself next time?" She coughed and leaned back over the bowl.

Lady Li rubbed her back and soothed her.

"I don't know," she said. "But we are going to find a doctor who can help you."

"I don't know if I can be helped," Swan said, shaking her head. "I don't even know who I am anymore."

Lady Li wasn't sure how to respond. She knew nothing of what Swan was going through. But she would do whatever it took to help her get well. She went to Swan's closet and found her some fresh clothes to wear. She helped her change and put her back into bed.

"I'll have cook bring you some hot broth," Lady Li said, tucking her in as she continued to shudder.

"Hello?" a voice called into the room.

Lady Li shot up and turned around, shocked to see Inspector Gong standing there.

"What are you doing?" she asked, rushing to the door to keep him from seeing Swan in her current state.

He backed out of the room to the courtyard. "I received your summons," he said. "But no one answered when I knocked at the gate, but it wasn't locked. Is something wrong?"

Lady Li sighed and motioned for him to follow her to the study. She must not have closed the gate properly when she came home, she was so shocked by the scene of her daughters running wild like monkeys.

"It has been...an eventful few hours," Lady Li said. "I have no idea where my servants even are right now. Forgive me for not having any hot water for tea right now."

"It's no bother," he said and turned her to face him. He placed both of his hands on her shoulders, and she felt a calming warmth rush through her body. "Tell me what's wrong."

"It is Swan," she said. "She is in desperate need of a doctor to help her with her opium addiction."

He frowned, but the nodded slowly. "What happened?"

"She had a large stash of opium hidden in her room," Lady Li explained. "But she doesn't remember taking it. She doesn't know how to stop even though she wants to. Eunuch Bai said there are doctors who can treat her, but we must proceed with discretion. Should your mother find out..."

"I know," he interrupted, releasing her and rubbing his chin. "I know someone I can trust. I'll send him over immediately."

"Thank you," she said. "Swan says that she—"

"You don't need to worry," Inspector Gong interrupted, stepping close to her and touching the side of her face. "I'll take care of everything."

She felt a shiver run from his fingers all the way down her spine. She remembered that only a few days before, they had made love like animals in this very room. Was he remembering that as well? As she looked up into his eyes and saw a hunger there, she thought that he must be. But that was before they had agreed he needed to marry Swan. Before he became a betrothed man. Before she had met with Swan's future in-laws.

Swan had been a dear friend to her for years. Someone she loved like a sister. Her face went hot with shame for the desire she felt for Swan's future husband.

She pulled her eyes away from his and stepped back.

"Thank you," she mumbled again. "Forgive me, but I am exhausted."

He did not pursue her but respected her excuse to put distance between them.

"Of course," he said. "I'll send for the doctor soon. Was there anything else?"

"No," she said, but then remembered her visit with Baoah. "Wait, yes. I met someone, a woman who was obsessed with Fanhua."

"Where?" he asked.

"Outside the theater as I was leaving last night," she said. "There must have been a dozen young ladies there hoping to catch a glimpse of him."

"I have heard that he was quite popular with the female patrons," he said. "Do you think one of these women might have had cause to harm him?"

"The young lady I met, Baoah," Lady Li said, "seemed to think not. She said they loved him. But I don't know. Many people kill those they love. If he betrayed one of the girls, or acted dishonorably in some way, it's possible."

"Indeed," the inspector said. "But who are these girls, and how would I contact them?"

"I don't know," Lady Li said, shaking her head, which now felt foggy. "You are right. It is too vague of an idea for now. I need more information. But she did mention another actor. She called him Hungjian. He is with the Xishan Szechuan Opera Troupe. She said he was also popular with women. Maybe they had a professional rivalry or something."

"I'll look into it," he said. He then made a move like he was going to step closer to her again, but then he stopped himself. "Anything else?"

"Not that I can think of right now," she said.

They both stood there in an awkward silence for several

moments before he finally gave a small bow and took his leave.

Lady Li sunk into a chair and felt faint. She didn't think it was because she was tired or hungry, but because a single look from Inspector Gong had the ability to render her completely powerless.

10

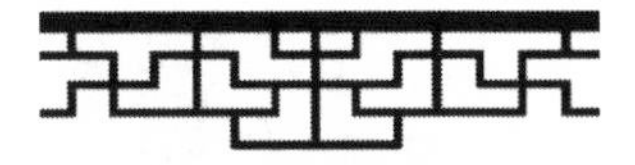

After Inspector Gong left Lady Li, he lingered outside her mansion gate for a moment. He wasn't sure why. He had things to do and there was nothing left to say to Lady Li, yet he couldn't seem to pull himself away. She drove him to distraction, where nothing else seemed to matter.

He finally remembered that he needed to go see Dr. Xue, both about Fanhua and Swan's opium addiction. He admitted that her addiction was a problem, but he wasn't sure if it would be worse for him if his mother found out before or after he married the girl. If his mother found out before, she would never approve the union. But if she found out after, she would never forgive him and would make Swan's life a living hell.

She would be right to do so, though, he had to admit. After all, what kind of a wife would Swan be if she was always in the clouds? She couldn't be a good mother in that state. But if Dr. Xue could cure her, everything would be fine, right?

He knew it wouldn't be. He was making a huge mistake.

But he couldn't back out now. Lady Li expected him to marry Swan. He couldn't disappoint her. Though, he doubted Lady Li truly wanted him to marry Swan. She wanted him. And it wasn't simply his overinflated opinion of himself that told him so. He could tell, even now, even after she refused to let him kiss or touch her, it was just as painful for her to push him away as it was for him to leave her. But what could they do? There was no way they could be together. It just wasn't possible...

Somehow, Inspector Gong found himself at Dr. Xue's shop, the scents of herbal medicines and dried sea creatures snapping him out of his thoughts before he was even standing in front of it. He stepped into the shop to find Dr. Xue talking to a male customer.

"What you need is ginko," Dr. Xue was telling the man. "These leaves here, they are already dried, so I'll grind them up for you, are from a tree in the north. An old, strong tree. Four thousand years old! You want your branch to be as thick and strong as that tree?" Dr. Xue and the man laughed as Dr. Xue put the leaves into a mortar and ground them up into a fine powder, which he then poured into a paper sachet.

"Just add it to a cup of tea one hour before bed," Dr. Xue instructed the man. "And take these peppers. You need more spicy food! Get the blood flowing. Have a hot dinner and then prepare for a hot night." They laughed again and the man gave Dr. Xue a few coins before slipping out of the shop.

"Will it work?" Inspector Gong asked as Dr. Xue cleaned off the counter.

"I'll give you some for your wedding night with Lady Yun and then you can tell me," Dr. Xue said tartly.

"How do you know about that?" Inspector Gong asked. "It's not official yet."

"You know your mother is a patient of mine," Dr. Xue said. "She was here looking for something she could slip into your tea to make you come to your senses."

"What did you give her?" Inspector Gong asked.

"Just some ground up lizard tails," he said, and Inspector Gong made a face. "Don't worry about it. Will just make your eyelids hairy."

"What?" Inspector Gong asked, grabbing a mirror off a nearby table and checking his face but not seeing any extra hairs. "Why would you do that?"

"Because I happen to be in agreement with her," Dr. Xue said. "This girl is not the one for you."

"I can never please anyone," Inspector Gong said with an annoyed sigh. "Both of you wanted me to get married, but the one I want is not good enough. She's a Manchu lady! I should be so lucky."

"But she's not the one that will be good for you," Dr. Xue said. "She's not the one that you stopped drinking and whoring for. She's not the one who opened your mind to the very idea of marriage. She's not the one who made you a better man. It's the other one."

"But I can't marry Lady Li," Inspector Gong said. "Besides, what does it matter? Who marries for love? I just need a woman who will give me sons, right?"

"For some men, that is enough," Dr. Xue said. "It was good enough for me. Be quiet, cook dinner, be big with child. What more would I need in a wife? But for you, you are not like me. You are a...What do they say? A romantic."

Inspector Gong shook his head. "I didn't come here to be insulted. And there's no point in arguing about this. It's out of my hands. I can't marry the woman I want, so any other woman will just have to do."

"When this all goes badly, you come back to me, you understand," Dr. Xue said. "You are like a son to me. I'll always help you."

"That's actually why I'm here," Inspector Gong said. "There is a problem with Swan. But don't you dare tell my mother. She can *never* know about this."

Dr. Xue raised an eyebrow. "Is she already with child?" he asked.

"No," Inspector Gong said. "She's addicted to opium."

He had expected Dr. Xue to rail at him, yell and throw things, tell him how stupid he was. But it was so quiet in that shop, he thought the whole neighborhood had frozen. Finally, Dr. Xue puckered his mouth tightly and tapped his long nails on the countertop.

"How much does she take?" he asked. "It is common for ladies, especially high-born ones, to imbibe once in a while, or to help them sleep. Is it more serious than that?"

"It is very serious," Inspector Gong said. "She sneaks out to go to opium houses. She had a large amount hidden in her room. She spends so much time in the clouds, she doesn't remember how she got there. And when she wakes up, she is sick."

Dr. Xue put his hand to his mouth, as though *he* was about to be sick over this knowledge. "You know this, yet you will marry her anyway?" he asked. Inspector Gong didn't reply. He had already said all he needed to on the matter. "I always took you for a fool, Anguo. I never thought you were stupid."

"Can you help her or not?" Inspector Gong asked.

Dr. Xue sighed and began rummaging around among the glass bottles under the counter. "Of course, I can help her," he mumbled. "I will have to take a very complicated three-prong approach. I have to balance her qi, help her manage her pain, and then flush the toxins from her body." He put several glass jars into a basket. "Hmm...snake venom, the good stuff..." He then went over to several baskets of herbs and put a few different items into paper sachets. "Ginseng...camellia..."

"Then what is the problem?" Inspector Gong asked. "If you can cure her, then everything will be fine, right?"

"I never said I could *cure* her," Dr. Xue huffed. "I can only *treat* her. I can help her survive today. I can heal her body from the damage the drug has already done. But the problem is her mind. She will always want to go back to the dreams. She will always find her way back there. You can never leave her alone. You can never trust her." He went back to collecting the items he needed such as milkwort leaves and pumpkin seeds.

"Maybe she is stronger than that," Inspector Gong said. "I'll give her a reason to fight."

"When your heart and mind are on another woman," Dr. Xue said, "how can you ever give Swan what she needs?"

"I promise to do my best by her," Inspector Gong said. "That's all I can do."

Dr. Xue sighed and finished putting items into the basket. "These treatments are expensive," he said. "And it will take a lot of my time."

"Don't worry about the cost," Inspector Gong said. "Whatever it takes. Just be discreet. We can't risk news about Swan's addiction getting back to my mother, or even circulating among the Manchu. It could hurt Lady Li's reputation as well."

"Fine, fine," Dr. Xue said. "I'll be sure to wear a hat. Anything else?"

"Have you had time to examine the body of the opera singer? Fanhua?" Inspector Gong asked.

"Yes, yes," Dr. Xue said. "Death was caused by a sword to the gut. Pierced the liver. Very painful but fast death."

"That explains why the blood darkened so quickly," Inspector Gong said. "How much force would it take to run someone through that way? She claims the murder was an accident."

"If the sword was very sharp, it could have happened very quickly," Dr. Xue said. "He was a thin boy. The bulk was in the costume, but it's just fabric and stuffing. Very easy to pierce. Still, very difficult to *accidentally* kill someone when you intentionally run them through with a sword."

"That is my viewpoint," Inspector Gong said. "But Prince Kung and Lady Li think the killer is not responsible for her actions. The singer said the prop sword was replaced with a real one, so she didn't realize until it was too late that she actually had injured him."

Dr. Xue nodded. "Very difficult case. But until you find out who switched the sword, I do not think you will find an answer."

"Yes, which is why I need to go. I have some leads to follow," the inspector said, heading for the door. "Let me know how things go with Swan."

The doctor only grunted as he locked the door to the shop behind him.

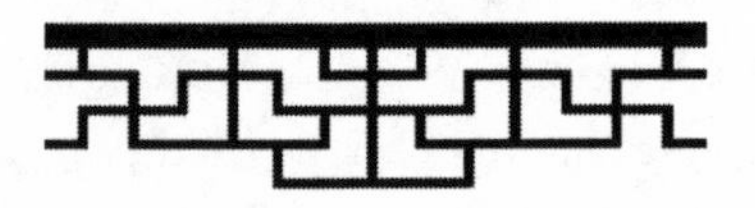

After some asking around, Inspector Gong easily found where Hungjian was currently performing. The Xishun troupe had rented the Green Willow Theater not far from the White Lotus Theater where Fanhua had been killed.

As he approached the theater, even though it was the middle of the day, he could hear loud music playing inside. At the door, there was a large man standing guard, and several women were anxiously trying to get inside. Inspector Gong elbowed his way through the crowd.

"No one is admitted during rehearsals," the guard growled, causing the girls to moan sadly.

"I'm here on the prince's business," Inspector Gong said, not needing to even give the name of the prince before being admitted. Inspector Gong's reputation preceded him.

Inspector Gong had never seen Szechuan opera before, so he was surprised by how different it was from Peking opera.

There was only one performer on stage, and he wasn't singing. There was a large orchestra off to one side, playing loud, upbeat music. The performer wore an ornate costume of black with gold and red embroidery. He wore a long black cape with a red silk lining and held a large red fan in one hand. He had a large black hat with shimmering baubles on it. His face looked as though it was painted red, black, and white.

With a flick of his wrist, the performer flashed the fan across his face, and his face was now green and white! Painted in a completely different pattern.

"What the..." Inspector Gong started to ask, but before he could form a full question, the performer turned his head to the left. Then back to the right. Now his face was red! In a split second, the man was able to completely change his face.

So, this was face changing, Inspector Gong realized with a laugh and clap of his hands. As the man moved commandingly around the stage, waving his fan or swinging his cape, he changed his face again and again before finally ending the act by revealing his real face. It was like a form a magic. Inspector Gong watched closely, trying to see how the man was able to change his face, but his movements were so quick, so seamless, he couldn't even begin to guess how it was done.

The man then took a bow and went to speak with the musicians on the side of the stage.

Inspector Gong clapped his hands as he approached the stage. "That was well done," he said as Hungjian looked at him. "I've never seen the like."

"The guard wasn't supposed to let anyone in," Hungjian said, hopping down off the stage and approaching the inspector. "I'm rehearsing a new act. No one was supposed to see it."

"Don't worry," Inspector Gong said. "I have no idea what I even just saw. I wouldn't begin to know how to explain it to someone."

"And you are?" the man asked, crossing his arms.

"Inspector Gong," he said.

Hungjian nodded slowly. "I've heard of you," he said. "But as we have had no crimes committed among our troupe, I assume you have come to talk about an acquaintance of mine. Tell me, what fool has run out and gotten himself killed?"

Inspector Gong hesitated. He hadn't planned on announcing the murder to anyone just yet. But this man was a competitor for attention—from women and opera patrons—with Fanhua. If anyone were the main suspect in Fanhua's murder, it would be Hungjian. His response to the news of Fanhua's death could tell the inspector everything he needed to know about him.

"Fanhua," was all Inspector Gong said.

Confusion crossed Hungjian's face. "What?" he asked, and then smiled, letting out a strangled laugh, as though Inspector Gong was playing a cruel joke. But then the truth of the matter dawned on him and the smile fled his face. "No," he gasped. He put his hand to his mouth as though he was going to be sick. He stumbled a bit. Then he turned his face away, and when he looked back, all emotion was gone. "That is unfortunate news," he said as though the inspector had only told him that it might rain.

Then the inspector realized that Hungjian was not merely an actor, but one skilled at changing his face and personality from one second to another. He wondered, which face was the real one? The one that had nearly gone to pieces a moment before, or the stoic and impassive one he was looking at now? He had no way of knowing. He began to doubt he'd be able to believe anything Hungjian had to say.

"How did it happen?" Hungjian asked.

Inspector Gong glanced around and noticed that the other troupe members were watching them, interested in whatever they were discussing.

"Perhaps we can talk somewhere more private?" the inspector asked.

"Of course," Hungjian said, and he led the inspector backstage to his dressing room, which, like the others the inspector had seen, was crowded with costumes and props.

"So, how do you do it?" the inspector asked, wanting to

distract Hungjian and get him comfortable talking. "The face changing. It's an impressive trick."

Hungjian chuckled as he took off his cape and hung it on a rack. "Do you think you are the first person to ask me that? It's a family secret, passed down through generations."

Inspector Gong nodded. Of course, Hungjian wasn't going to reveal his tricks. "I'm finding there are many secrets to the opera world," he said. "Perhaps you will reveal to me your rivalry with Fanhua."

The inspector couldn't be sure, but he thought he saw a hint of sadness cross Hungjian's face again before he once again masked his feelings.

"There was no rivalry, not really," he said. "It was just for show. It made the admirers more enthralled if they thought there was some sort of competition going on between us. It made both of us more popular. But as I am sure you have seen, our styles are completely different. There could never be a real rivalry."

"It might not have been real to you," the inspector said. "But it was very real to the women who loved him. Could one of your admirers have killed him to help you?"

"What?" Hungjian asked. "That's crazy."

"From what I have heard, Fanhua made the girls crazy," the inspector said. "Who knows what a woman might do if she thought Fanhua loved her."

"If anything, those girls would have killed Wangshu," Hungjian said. "*She* made them crazy."

"In what way?" the inspector asked.

"Those women are obsessed with Fanhua because he played a woman," Hungjian explained. "When he had to play a man, their world was shattered. It was as if they were all forced to suddenly awaken from a dream."

"But if Fanhua had been leading a girl on," the inspector

said. "Teasing her. It would make sense for a girl to turn on him and—"

"It wasn't Fanhua!" Hungjian suddenly snapped.

The inspector stopped talking and waited for Hungjian to continue.

Hungjian hesitated, shaking his head in disgust at himself for breaking character.

"Fanhua went along with the rivalry, but he didn't get close to the girls," he said. "He...he was a cut sleeve. And he was a good actor, but he couldn't pretend to love the girls. He wanted to be one of them. He only loved men."

A cut sleeve referred to a story about male love from hundreds of years ago. It was a term often used to talk about men who only loved men. Having spent years in the military, Inspector Gong was no stranger to men who occasionally had relations with men. But most men who had relations with men were not cut sleeves. Most would go on to marry women and do their duty by their families by siring sons. A cut sleeve was someone who would not do this but could only sate their passions with other men.

Inspector Gong wasn't sure at first how to respond to this information. The idea that Fanhua was not just a cut sleeve but wanted to *be* a woman was something he couldn't quite wrap his head around.

"About these men he loved," the inspector said slowly. "Would any of them have cause to hurt Fanhua?"

Hungjian cleared his throat and shook his head. "I don't think so. Many of his patrons would simply loose interest in him if he didn't play the part of the dan."

"Why are you so sure of this?" Inspector Gong asked. "How do you know so much about Fanhua's...private life?"

Hungjian smiled and was back to the careless actor he so wanted to portray. "Oh, there are few secrets backstage in the opera world. And we were friends. There is little about Fanhua that I don't know."

"Except who would have killed him?" Inspector Gong needled, trying to goad Hungjian into another reaction, but Hungjian held onto his role for dear life.

"Except that," Hungjian conceded. "A true tragedy. He was the most exquisite dan. Quite a loss to the opera world."

"And to you?" Inspector Gong pressed.

"Of course," Hungjian said innocently. "He was a dear friend, and I shall mourn him for years to come."

Inspector Gong inwardly groaned in annoyance. Apparently, Hungjian had completely gained control over this face he wanted to present and was not going to let go. He wasn't going to get any more useful information out of this face changer for now.

"If you can think of anything else that will be useful," the inspector said, "send for me."

"Of course, inspector," Hungjian said with a smile.

The inspector left in annoyance. He couldn't trust anything Hungjian said. The part about Fanhua being a cut sleeve was probably true, but it was a strange thing for Hungjian to be upset about if he didn't have some sort of relationship beyond friendship with Fanhua himself. But the cold way he was able to hide his true feelings on the matter unnerved Inspector Gong.

Which made him think of Wangshu and how he couldn't trust anything she said either. He realized that trying to wrangle information out of such skilled actors was becoming his least favorite way to try to find a killer.

But he had the killer. And her name was Wangshu. Lady Li and Prince Kung might want him to lay the blame on someone else, but if he couldn't cut through the lies and find someone else, it was Wangshu's head that would roll.

He decided to go back to the White Lotus Theater and confront Wangshu with the true perils of her situation. One way or another, he would scare the truth out of her. If she wanted to keep her head, she needed to tell him the truth.

Inspector Gong entered the theater and went right to Wangshu's dressing room. He tried to open the door without even knocking, but the room was locked.

"Wangshu!" he demanded as he shook the door handle. "Open up. We need to talk." He looked around, wondering where the guard the prince had assigned to Wangshu had gone.

Some of the other troupe members peeked down the hall at the inspector.

"Does anyone have a key?" he asked. The onlookers all shook their heads. The inspector groaned and assessed the door. It looked rather flimsy. He stood back and kicked at the handle. Once, twice, and the handle gave way and the door swung open.

Wangshu was not in the room, and many of the costumes he had seen strewn about before were also gone.

Just as he knew would happen the moment Lady Li and the prince asked him not to take Wangshu into custody, the murderess had fled.

11

Lady Li sat by Swan's side and tried to coax her into drinking some broth.

"It tastes like sawdust," Swan said through her dry, cracking throat.

"That's because you've been filling your mouth with so much smoke," Lady Li replied as he held up another spoonful.

Swan pushed the spoon away and retched into the bowl by her bed again. She leaned back on her pillow, panting.

Lady Li placed her hand on Swan's forehead, which was burning up. "Your future husband is sending for a doctor," Lady Li said. "I'm sure he will be here soon."

"My future husband," Swan repeated dreamily. "I can't believe this is happening."

"It will only happen if you get well," Lady Li said, putting the broth and spoon aside.

"Does it hurt you?" Swan asked. "To know that I will marry Inspector Gong and not you?"

Lady Li pressed her lips and her brow furrowed. She wasn't sure why Swan was trying to get a rise out of her, but she wouldn't lower herself by losing her temper with a sick woman. She tucked the covers in around Swan's frail body and took some satisfaction in knowing that Inspector Gong wouldn't take nearly as much pleasure in Swan's bony frame as he did in her own more shapely one.

"It was my decision," Lady Li said.

Swan smirked. "You didn't answer my question."

Lady Li sighed and shook her head. "What does it matter?" she asked.

"How can I be happy in a new marriage knowing that it causes you pain?" Swan asked.

A flood of guilt washed over Lady Li. Swan hadn't asked the question to hurt her, but to alleviate her own guilt over having the chance at a new family, a new life, and leaving Lady Li behind. Lady Li was so jealous and had been acting so petty, she thought that Swan must be envious and vindictive as well.

Lady Li sat on the bed and took Swan's hand in her own. "Meimei," she said, emphasizing that she saw Swan as not just her late husband's concubine, but her own sister, "you and I have both been wronged. We should never have been widowed so young. But our similarities end there. As a first wife, I must stay as I am. I must protect my daughters. But you have another chance. You can escape this life. Don't think about me. Escape while you can."

Swan started to cry and put her hand to her eyes. "The only escape for me has been in the clouds," she said. "I cannot imagine ever being happy in this world."

"Yes, you can!" Lady Li insisted. "Once you are married to Inspector Gong, everything will change for you! You will be an honored first wife in a large family with many sisters-in-law and nieces and nephews. Your husband will take his pleasure with you and you will have children of your own."

"But what if I can't?" Swan asked, sitting up. "I lost my baby. My son! If Inspector Gong knew—"

"Shut your mouth, you idiot!" Lady Li said harshly, looking around as if Inspector Gong or his mother might suddenly manifest. "When a woman has twenty years to birth a dozen children, it is very common to lose one or two. It doesn't mean you can't still have many healthy children."

"Then why are we keeping it a secret," Swan asked. "If Inspector Gong knew the truth, he wouldn't marry me, would he?"

"What do you want me to do?" Lady Li asked. "You are right. He wouldn't. But I want you married. I want you happy. Keeping this thing a secret is the only way. If you want, after you have a healthy son, then you can tell him about the one you lost. He is a reasonable man. He will understand why you didn't tell him. But then it won't matter."

"But what if I never have a son?" Swan asked. "What if I can't?"

"Then he will take a concubine," Lady Li said. "And she can birth children for you. You'll still be a first wife, which will be a much better life than you are living now."

Swan leaned back again and sighed, her eyelids droopy. "I hope you are right," she said. The conversation seemed to have drained her of whatever energy she had, and she was quickly asleep once again.

Lady Li turned toward the door and was not at all surprised to see Eunuch Bai standing there. He lowered his head and backed away as she left the room and closed the door.

"Do you need something?" she asked softly so as not to disturb Swan.

He handed her a folded piece of paper with the empress's seal on it. "You've been summoned."

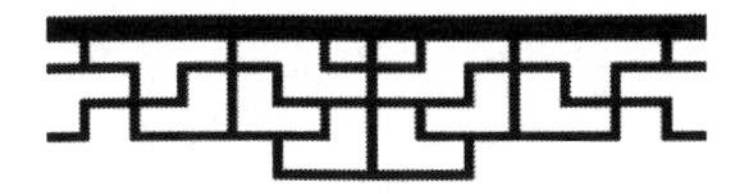

Lady Li hadn't seen the empress in several months. Not since they found out who had murdered her sister-in-law, who had been serving as one of the empress's ladies-in-waiting, though they had sent each other letters many times.

When she arrived at the Forbidden City, she was shown directly into the empress's sitting room. The empress was seated in her chair, smoking her water pipe, several of her ladies seated around her on lower stools working on their embroidery.

Te-hai, the empress's chief eunuch—and Lady Li suspected much more—announced her arrival. The empress and the ladies all stood, but only the ladies bowed to Lady Li, acknowledging her superior status. Lady Li nodded to the girls, and then did a lady's kowtow to the empress, one in which she kneeled on one knee as opposed to knocking her forehead to the floor.

"Leave us," the empress ordered the ladies and eunuchs. They all did, except for Te-hai, who lingered near the door. The empress could never be completely alone.

Lady Li squeezed the empress's hand as they sat close together. "How are you, dear friend?"

"I'm quite well," the empress said. "Prince Kung told me that you were at Wangshu's debut performance. You must tell me all about it."

"Wh-what did the prince tell you?" Lady Li stammered. She did not want to be the person to have to tell the empress that Wangshu killed someone her first night on stage.

The empress pouted. "Oh, you know him. Always too busy for me." Lady Li doubted that. If Prince Kung had time for anyone, it was the empress, but she nodded in commiseration. "He told me to ask you since you saw it as well. What happened?"

"She was wonderful," Lady Li said honestly. "It is so inspiring to see a woman on stage. Male dans are talented, to be sure, but there was something so...believable about Wangshu's performance."

The empress leaned back and draped her arm over her head dramatically. "I so wish I could have seen it for myself."

"But you've seen her many times," Lady Li said. "She's part of your private troupe."

"It's not the same as seeing her perform in a real theater, in front of hundreds of patrons," the empress said. "What about the crowd? Did they love her?"

"Eventually," Lady Li said. "They heckled her at first. Booing and hissing. But she was so professional. She continued her performance perfectly and eventually, no one could resist being enraptured by her."

The empress sighed. "Incredible. You think people will be more accepting of female performers in the future?"

"One can hope," Lady Li hedged, but the empress must have sensed her reticence.

"What?" the empress asked. "What aren't you telling me?"

"I don't know what you mean," Lady Li said, but she knew the empress was on to something, like a tiger who smelled blood.

The empress stared Lady Li down with dark eyes that had broken men with just a glance, but Lady Li continued playing dumb. Finally, the empress slapped Lady Li's leg.

"Meimei!" she yelled. "Tell me!"

"You're only going to be angry," Lady Li said, shaking her head.

"I have simpering toadies around me all day only telling me what they think I want to hear," the empress said. "You are the only person I can trust to tell me the truth, so out with it! Did she miss her cues? Did she fall off the stage? Did she lose her voice? Was she terrible?"

"No," Lady Li said with a sigh, shaking her head. "She was wonderful, I promise you."

"Then what is the problem?" the empress asked.

"You know the opera? The story of it, I mean," Lady Li said.

"Of course," the empress replied.

"There is a scene where Xueyan kills the general," she said. "Where she runs him through with a sword."

"Yes, I know," the empress said anxiously, waiting for Lady Li to get to the point.

"To make the scene look real, the troupe used a fake sword, one that would collapse when Wangshu stabbed Fanhua," Lady Li said. The empress nodded. "Well, someone switched the swords. Wangshu used a real sword in that scene."

She paused, and the two women looked at each other for a moment.

"And..." the empress pushed, not understanding what Lady Li was trying to tell her.

"So...Wangshu really killed Fanhua," Lady Li finally said, squinting in expectation of the empress's wrath. But the wrath didn't come. It took far too long for the empress to finally comprehend what Lady Li had said.

"How...what?" the empress finally asked. "On stage? During the actual performance? Wangshu...*killed* Fanhua?"

Lady Li nodded. "I'm afraid it's true. I saw it and spoke to her after the show."

"Then why isn't it in all the papers?" the empress asked. "Where is Wangshu? Has she been arrested?"

"No one other than myself, Prince Kung, and Inspector Gong seemed to realize that the general was really dead," Lady Li said. "The audience all thought it was just part of the show."

"It must have been an incredible show, if people thought the death was only part of it," the empress said. "So what happened? Where is Wangshu now?"

"She's still staying in her room at the theater while Inspector Gong investigates," Lady Li said.

"Investigates what?" the empress asked. "If you saw Wangshu kill the poor boy, what is the inspector looking for?"

"He is looking for the real killer," Lady Li said. "Wangshu said she had no reason to kill Fanhua. Someone else switched the swords. Someone else wanted Wangshu to kill Fanhua and frame her for the murder."

"Are you sure?" the empress asked. "Seems very complicated to me."

"I...hmm," Lady Li said. Actually, she couldn't be sure that Wangshu didn't kill Fanhua on purpose and then made up the story about the sword being switched. She wanted to believe Wangshu, but she supposed that Inspector Gong's investigation would only lead him back to Wangshu. "It is possible that Wangshu killed Fanhua on purpose," Lady Li admitted. "But we need to be sure. We can't let the Ministry of Justice execute an innocent woman."

"Oh, wouldn't that just please every man in this city if the first female opera singer was executed," the empress said, squeezing her clawed fingers into fists. "This is a direct attack on me, you know."

It was typical of the empress to turn the murder of a young man by an innocent woman into a personal attack on her. But the more Lady Li thought about it, she supposed it was possible. The empress was making a political statement by sanctioning the first public opera performance by a woman. Having that woman then publicly executed would, in turn, also be a political statement. One saying that women were to be neither seen nor heard. And that women were certainly not meant to rule.

"That isn't the angle the inspector is pursuing at this time," Lady Li said, "but I will bring the possibility to his attention."

"That poor girl," the empress said. "She must be terrified. I should never have let her leave the palace."

"You can't keep her locked up forever," Lady Li said, using the same voice she did when counseling her children. "When this all blows over, the city will thank you for sharing her. Who knows, maybe the entire opera world will change after this. Can you imagine if all women's parts were played by women?"

"I imagine it all the time," the empress said. She stood up and rushed over to her desk, pulling out a stack of papers. "Look at what I have written," she said.

Lady Li walked over to see what the empress was so

excited about. "*The Manchu Daughters of the Lord of the Manor*," the title read. She skimmed the rest of the page. "This is an opera, but one I haven't seen before."

"Because I wrote it!" the empress said. "And every character is a woman. From the daughters to the mothers to the servants. Men, like the manor lord, are referenced but never seen on stage. What do you think?"

Lady Li was intrigued by the idea of an all-female opera. There were some plays that had largely female casts, such as *The Generals of the Yang Family*, but, of course, the female characters had always been played by men. An opera about women, written by a woman, and performed by women? The mere thought made Lady Li's heart beat fast in her chest.

"This is very exciting," Lady Li said. "One day I hope you will be known as a great empress and a great playwright."

"But first your Inspector Gong will have to find the real killer," the empress said.

Lady Li blushed at the empress calling him *her* Inspector Gong, but she quickly calmed herself and nodded.

"I will do my best to help him," she said.

12

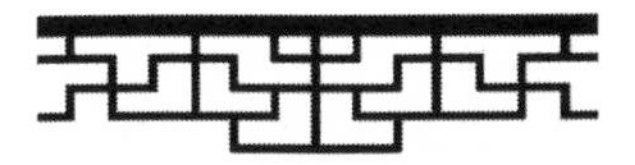

Even though the room looked less cluttered with the elaborate costumes gone, the room seemed even more out of order. The dressing table was askew and the stool knocked over. The sleeping couch had been moved as well. It almost appeared to the inspector that there had been a struggle, yet there was something off about it. Could Wangshu have been kidnapped? Would a kidnapper have taken the costumes as well? He wasn't sure.

It made more sense to Inspector Gong that Wangshu would take the costumes. They had to be quite expensive. If she hoped to survive somewhere else as an opera singer, she would need the costumes. Or she could sell them and have money to survive until she found some other way to earn money. The problem was he had no idea where she might have gone. She could be holed up in an inn somewhere or she might have just fled the city completely. It was possible she could have returned to the empress at the Forbidden City. That might be the smartest thing for her to do. As head of the Inner Court, the empress could simply take Wangshu in as one of her ladies and no one could say anything about it, not even the prince or the Ministry of Justice.

He never did finish interviewing the other members of the opera troupe, so he thought now might as well be the best time. He might even learn something about Wangshu that would tell him where she might have gone.

"This is a disgrace!"

The voice of the Lord of Hell boomed through the opera hall, even backstage where the inspector was.

"The people deserve better," the Lord of Hell lamented. "The death and destruction have gone on too long..."

Inspector Gong made his way to the side of the stage and watched as the head of the troupe, Changpu, raised himself up to his full height and held his arm out in front of him. He took a deep breath and then belted out the first long note of the solo he was practicing. The other players cowered before the Lord of Hell as the musicians pounded on drums. Even without the makeup and costumes, the practice performance was powerful. The inspector decided to watch the rehearsal for a few minutes.

"No, no, no," Changpu said, interrupting his own performance, his face scowling as he stomped over to the musicians and started explaining to them how they were playing the song wrong.

Inspector Gong clapped as he made his way onto the stage. "I thought it was a fantastic performance."

Changpu waved him off. "Only because you don't know any better."

The inspector chuckled as he stepped up to the other players. "Why didn't you have Wangshu join you."

"She wasn't needed for this scene," one of the men replied.

"Good thing," the inspector said. "Because she's gone."

"What?" Changpu demanded as the other actors looked at each other confused. "What do you mean she's gone? Where has she gone?"

"I don't know," the inspector said coolly. "I rather hoped you could tell me. All of her costumes are missing as well."

"Why that little..." Changpu's voice trailed off as he stomped backstage.

"First our wusheng, now our dan," one of the other actors said.

"I always said having her here was a curse," said one of the others as the other concurred with a nod of their heads.

"Hold on," the inspector said. "Let me have your names first, then you can tell me about Wangshu's...curse."

"I'm Kangjun," the first man said, who was tall and skinny. "This is Laquan," he said pointing to the man next to him who actually looked no older than a teenager. "And that's Pingru." Pingru looked to be the oldest of the three, but not by much. Inspector Gong suspected the boy only looked a little older because he had a bit more roundness to him.

"Okay, Kangjun," the inspector said. "Tell me about Wangshu."

Kangjun scoffed and shook his head. "It was wrong to take her on," he said firmly. "It's a perversion, letting a woman strut around, displaying herself in front of all manner of men. Disgusting. I'd never marry a girl like that."

"But the troupe was ordered by the empress to take her on," the inspector said. "Changpu didn't have much of a choice."

"Anyone's morals are for sale for the right price," he said. "If we hadn't taken her on, some other troupe would have, but at least we would have had the moral high ground."

"So why would someone kill Fanhua and not Wangshu if Wangshu was the one acting improperly?" the inspector asked.

The three shrugged their shoulders and looked down at their feet. The inspector thought they must know something they weren't telling him.

"We can talk about this at the Ministry of Justice instead, if you like," he said.

"No!" Laquan said. "Wangshu is the killer. We were all watching when she did it."

"How do you know that?" the inspector said. "You weren't on stage at the time."

"But we were all watching her," he said. "Ask anyone. Her performance...it was incredible! You heard her. Voice of a fairy. It was like...she bewitched anyone who listened to her."

"She had you under her spell, did she?" the inspector asked with a chuckle in his voice.

"Well, maybe not me," the boy said shyly. "She never looked at me for more than two seconds. But everyone else, they loved her and hated her. You can't deny her singing ability, the way she commanded the stage. She was a natural performer. But it wasn't right! Women shouldn't be in the public eye. 'When the hen announces the dawn, it signals the demise of the family,'" he quoted.

Inspector Gong had always scoffed at that particular admonition. He knew from experience that it was always a woman who awoke first in the morning to light the fires while the men waited until the room was warm before rising. It was the same in most families, he was sure. But he understood the boy's meaning. Many people would have been offended by the idea of a woman speaking, not to mention singing and performing, in public. But none of that explained why Fanhua was dead and not Wangshu. He kept coming back to this central problem.

"Everyone loved her?" the inspector asked. "What about Fanhua?"

Pingru let out what could almost be described as a belly laugh. "Certainly not Fanhua."

"Why not?" the inspector asked. "Because she stole his role as the dan?"

"Sure, that was part of it," Pingru said. "Fanhua was born to play a dan. It's the only role he's good at. You saw it. He was a terrible wusheng."

The inspector didn't know why everyone kept saying that. He thought Fanhua was just fine as a wusheng, but what did he know about opera, really?

"What was the other part?" he asked. "Why else did Fanhua not like Wangshu?"

The three players shuffled their feet again.

"Was it because he preferred men?" the inspector offered.

"So you know?" Pingru said and then nodded. "Good."

"Did it offend Wangshu that Fanhua was a cut sleeve?" the inspector asked.

"I don't think she was here long enough to realize," Pingru said. "She knew he was mad at her for taking his role, so she was always flirting with him, giving him food and silks as gifts to placate him. He was upset over losing the role, but always having her close to him, touching him, it just made things worse between them."

"Did he insult her? Hurt her in some way?" the inspector asked. "Could there have been strain between them enough for Wangshu to want him dead?"

The three looked at each other and then laughed.

"On opening night?" Kangjun asked. "In front of

hundreds of people? What was her plan then? If she wanted to be the only dan there are easier ways than ending up with your head chopped off."

The inspector began to feel a fire in his belly as his irritation grew. This case was simply impossible.

"What about anyone else in the troupe?" he asked through gritted teeth. "Would anyone else want Fanhua dead? Did anyone find his relationship with men offensive?"

The three shook their heads.

"Women love the men who play the dan," Kangjun said. "That is always the case for every troupe. But also, in most troupes, the dan only loves men. It is...almost natural."

"Natural?" the inspector asked, raising an eyebrow.

"I believe that men who are drawn to play the role of a woman," Laquan said, "were born in the wrong body. They have the spirit of a woman. It is why they play them so convincingly."

"And why women are drawn to them," Pingru added. "Even if the women don't understand it."

"What about the female admirers?" the inspector asked, trying one last line of questioning. "They hated Wangshu as well, correct? Could any of them be behind this?"

"Many of Fanhua's followers were upset that he was no longer playing the dan," Kangjun said. "And they blamed Wangshu for that. Wangshu was scared to leave the theater without a disguise because she thought the other women might attack her. They loved Fanhua. I can't imagine any of them hurting him."

Neither could Inspector Gong. He was feeling near the end of his rope. He saw Changpu return to the stage, so he dismissed the three younger actors and approached the troupe leader.

"What do you think?" Inspector Gong asked.

"That little bitch," Changpu spat. "I'm going to have to cancel the upcoming shows. Even if I could find a new wusheng and dan, she took some of the best costumes. It will cost a fortune to replace what was stolen."

"Don't cancel anything yet," the inspector said. "If you do, people will know something happened to Wangshu, if not Fanhua."

"What am I supposed to do with no performers or costumes?" Changpu asked.

"You were going to have to find a new wusheng anyway," the inspector said. "Keep auditioning new players. Let me look for Wangshu. If I find her, hopefully I will find the missing costumes as well. Where do you think she might have gone?"

"Back to the empress, I suppose," Changpu said. "I'm going to send her a letter right now. It is her fault the little dog was sent here, and it has brought me nothing but grief. The loss of my wusheng, the low ticket sales, now the loss of costumes and canceled shows. The empress should pay dearly for this."

The inspector couldn't help but somewhat agree. If the empress hadn't been so intent getting seeing a woman on stage, none of this would have happened. The empress had upset the social order, and now countless people would pay the price. She should have left well enough alone.

"Now that you have had more time to think about it," the inspector asked, hoping to get an honest answer while Changpu was ruffled, "who do you think killed your nephew?"

"I wish I knew," Changpu said. "It has been the constant question in my mind. The only answer I have is Wangshu. She and Fanhua were at odds and she did the deed.

Though, that she should be so angry with Fanhua as to kill him is simply beyond me. I never would have suspected..." He seemed to be at a loss for words and simply shook his head.

The inspector didn't blame him. There seemed to be no clear motive for the crime. Though this would not be the first murder he had come across where the motive was less than clear. Sometimes people just killed each other. Whether they snapped, felt a sense of power from it, or were simply insane—the truth of the matter was that humans sometimes acted in a way that defied all logic or understanding.

"If you do think of anything else," the inspector said, "let me know."

Changpu nodded and then headed to his office, most likely to write his scathing letter to the empress.

Inspector Gong headed backstage, back to Wangshu's dressing room. He wanted to take a look at it one more time in case she had left behind a clue as to where she might have gone. But as he entered the hallway, he saw a cloaked figure crouched before Fanhua's door. The person laid a bouquet of flowers on the ground and placed a hand on the door.

The inspector wondered who it was. A fan who found out that Fanhua had died? A heartbroken lover? He couldn't be sure. He took a step forward, hoping to get a better look, but he accidentally nudged a box of props, making a scraping sound.

The cloaked figure looked up at the inspector, but the face was dark, so the inspector couldn't see who it was.

"You there," the inspector called out with a commanding voice, taking a large step toward the person, hoping to intimidate him—or her—into staying put.

But it didn't work. The person turned away and bolted down the hallway.

The inspector cursed under his breath as he chased after the person. But he wasn't quick enough. But the time he reached the end of the hallway and rounded the corner, the cloaked figure was gone.

13

"Tell me about your eldest daughter," the empress said to Lady Li as she was about to take her leave.

"She is well," Lady Li said, unable to hide a hint of pride in her voice. "She is excelling at her studies and growing taller every day I believe."

"The next time you come see me," the empress said, "you must bring her with you. After all, I could be her mother-in-law one day."

Lady Li's heart nearly fell into her stomach at the empress's words. For First Daughter to one day be an imperial consort had long been her life's ambition, but to hear the empress speak so plainly of the possibility for the first time, she was surprised that she didn't feel excitement in her chest, but fear.

"Of...of course, my lady," Lady Li said with a bow. "I am sure she would love to visit the palace."

"Perhaps my son could be present as well," the empress said, leaning in and whispering conspiratorially. It was not common for young men and women—even imperial ones

—to meet one another before their wedding day, unless they happened to grow up together.

"It would be interesting to see how they get along," Lady Li said.

"Quite right," the empress said. "Gods forbid they actually know one another and find each other pleasing before they are forced to marry."

"And if they can't stand each other?" Lady Li asked jokingly but was genuinely concerned.

"Who wouldn't instantly love your charming child?" the empress asked. "And who wouldn't love the emperor? No, it will be a match ordained by Heaven!"

Lady Li tried to smile but felt her lips quiver at the thought. She remembered the last time she was here in the Forbidden City, when she was helping Inspector Gong find out who killed her sister-in-law, Suyi. She had learned that the palace was full of sorrow for the women trapped within the walls, walls that held terrible secrets.

Even though she had always dreamed that one day her daughter might be the next empress of China, she knew that such a life was truly only one of misery. Could she really sentence her daughter to that life?

Did she have a choice?

Lady Li kneeled before the empress. "My lady, my dear friend, thank you for summoning me, but I am afraid I have many pressing matters to attend at home."

"Of course," the empress said sadly.

Lady Li knew that the empress had few confidants, few real friends in the palace, but she couldn't linger. She needed to see to Swan, and she felt a pressing urge to rush home and hold her daughters close to her chest.

"I will alert you to any updates on Wangshu," Lady Li said.

"Please do," the empress said. "And let me know if there is anything I can do to help her."

Lady Li nodded and then took her leave. She wasn't sure what the empress could do to help, but such an offer was not one to take lightly.

As she rode home in her sedan chair, she knew she should be thinking about the murder and how to help Wangshu, but she found herself more worried about First Daughter's future. But if the empress and the grand councilors selected First Daughter to be a consort, there wasn't anything she could do about it. It wasn't an offer she would be able to refuse. And why should she want to? Was it not what every Manchu woman dreamed of? One day being the most powerful woman in the country? Yet she couldn't shake the gnawing dread growing in the put of her stomach.

When she arrived home, it was early evening, and her daughters were already having their dinner. She walked up behind them and kissed them both on the tops of their heads.

"What's wrong with Auntie Swan?" First Daughter asked, not even noticing her mother being near to tears.

"What do you mean?" Lady Li asked.

"There is a doctor in her room," Second Daughter explained. "Is she sick?"

"Perhaps a bit," Lady Li said, not wanting to alarm them. "But I am sure it is nothing serious."

The girls nodded, unconcerned, and went back to eating. Lady Li tried to convince herself she was just being overly emotional with regards to her daughters and forced her concerns deep inside as she went to check on Swan.

The door to Swan's room was open and Eunuch Bai was standing watch. Lady Li gasped when she looked into the room. Swan was lying face down on a couch completely naked save for a silk sheet covering the lower half of her body. She had acupuncture needles sticking out from her neck, shoulders, arms, and along her spine. A pungent incense was burning and some tea was brewing in a small pot.

"This is highly inappropriate!" Lady Li snapped, but the old man who was hovering over Swan administering the acupuncture shushed her.

"Do you want her to be cured or not?" he asked in a low voice.

"Of course, I do!" Lady Li said. "But Inspector Gong can't have known that this is what you meant, for you to be seeing so much of his bride."

"He told me to heal her by any means necessary," the doctor said. "And believe me, this is necessary. The opium has infected every part of her body."

"But—" Lady Li started to protest again.

"I have been supervising the entire time to make sure nothing...untoward happened," Eunuch Bai interrupted.

Lady Li sighed but said no more for the moment. She would have to let the doctor do his work. Thankfully, he had been nearly done when she arrived. He removed the acupuncture needles and covered Swan completely with the sheet, but she didn't move.

The doctor then poured a cup of the tea and set it on a small table by the couch. "When she wakes, make sure she drinks this," he said. He then handed several small sachets to Eunuch Bai. "The instructions are on each one. Make sure the directions are followed exactly. I will return tomorrow and every day this week to perform more acupuncture."

Eunuch Bai took the sachets and motioned for a maid to help dress Swan and move her back to her bed. Lady Li walked the doctor to the gate.

"Thank you for coming, and for your assistance," Lady Li said. "It was simply a shock to find you here, and to see Swan in such a state."

The doctor nodded. "I understand. I know you have been helping Inspector Gong with the strange murder at the theater."

"Do you?" Lady Li asked, raising an eyebrow.

"I examined the body of the young man," the doctor explained. "But there was nothing unusual about it."

"I suppose you are the person who examined Yun Suyi's body as well," Lady Li said. "Thank you for taking such care with her."

The doctor nodded. "I am Dr. Xue, Lady Li. I think you and I have been working together for some time without realizing it thanks to our mutual friend."

"I guess so," Lady Li said with a small smile.

"I have known the inspector for many years," the doctor said as they approached the gate. "I was quite glad to know he had finally heeded my advice and was looking for a wife."

Lady Li didn't respond, she was so surprised by the turn the conversation had taken.

"But I was quite dismayed when I discovered *who* he would be marrying," he continued.

"Dr. Xue," Lady Li said with an exhausted sigh. "I appreciate your concern—"

"I'm sure you don't," Dr. Xue interrupted. "But if he won't listen to me, perhaps you will. This marriage cannot go forward."

"If it were up to Inspector Gong," Lady Li corrected, "he wouldn't marry her either. He has made his...affection for me clear. I am the one who insists he look for a companion elsewhere. There is simply no future for us together, so he needs to move on with his life."

"Lady Li—" the doctor started to say but was interrupted by a pounding on the gate.

Since she was there, Lady Li opened the door herself and was shocked to see Wangshu there, along with several large bags.

"I...I didn't know where else to go," Wangshu said.

"Of course," Lady Li said ushering her inside and helping her with her bags. "I'm sorry, doctor. Perhaps we could *not* finish this conversation another time."

The doctor chuckled and showed himself out. "Until tomorrow, my lady."

"I'm sorry to intrude if someone is ill," Wangshu said.

Lady Li waved her off and motioned for a maid to assist with the bags. "It is nothing," she said. "I'll have the servants prepare a room for you. Let's have some hot tea while we wait." She pulled Wangshu by the arm toward the dining room where her daughters were finishing up their evening meal.

When Wangshu entered the room, Second Daughter's eyes lit up and she ran over to her with her mouth hanging open.

"You are the beautiful opera singer I saw the other night," Second Daughter exclaimed.

Wangshu kneeled down to Second Daughter's level. "I am," she said. "Did you enjoy the show?"

"Oh yes!" Second Daughter said. She waved her fingers left and right and did a little spin. Lady Li couldn't help but laugh at how poised her daughter was. "I've been practicing. I want to be an opera singer just like you!"

"Well, that makes it almost worthwhile, doesn't it?" Wangshu asked with a hint of sadness in her voice.

"Come, come," Lady Li said, moving her daughter out of the way so Wangshu could sit in one of the chairs. "Have some tea. Are you hungry?"

"Famished," Wangshu said. "I've been walking, dragging those bags for hours. I wasn't sure where to go."

"Why are you here at all?" Lady Li asked. "Why didn't you stay at the theater?"

One of the servants brought Wangshu a bowl of rice and a pair of chopsticks, along with a cup of hot tea. The dishes of food were still on the table from when the girls had been eating. They also brought a bowl for Lady Li, who had quite forgotten the last time she had eaten as well.

"The theater isn't safe for me anymore," Wangshu said, shaking her head. "I have received so many hateful letters, telling me that I am a whore, an abomination for being on the stage." She gasped and looked at the two little girls. "I'm sorry to say such things. I'm not in my right mind."

"No, don't concern yourself," Lady Li said, motioning with her chopsticks for Wangshu to eat. "I know this has been a difficult time for you."

"Today was the worst of it," Wangshu said, tears welling in her eyes. "A man broke into my room. He was waiting for me after rehearsal. He said he was going to punish me for not knowing my place. I screamed, but no one came! The rest of the troupe, they despise me, I know it!"

Lady Li was beginning to regret not sending her daughters away as Wangshu told her story.

"He pushed me backward and I tripped over a stool," Wangshu continued. "But I stood and ran behind my couch to get away from him. He grabbed me and tossed me against the wall by my dresser. I reached down, grabbed a hairpin, and stabbed him in the shoulder with it!"

Lady Li and both of her daughters winced as Wangshu imitated the stabbing action, her eyes wild.

"He yelled, calling me dirty names," Wangshu said. "And then he stumbled out of my room and down the hallway. I was so scared. I was out of my mind and didn't know where to go. I threw everything into my bags and left. But you were so kind to me, Lady Li. Defending me against that cruel inspector. I knew you would help me. So I asked around if anyone knew where you lived, and thankfully it wasn't far. I don't know that I could have carried those bags much further."

"I am so sorry that happened to you," Lady Li said, reaching over and gripping Wangshu's hand. "What happened to the guard the prince left for you?"

Wangshu's mouth opened, but she did not immediately reply. "He...he must have left," she finally said. "I don't know. Maybe the attacker bribed him or something."

Lady Li doubted someone could have offered a bribe big enough to be worth the man's life. If the prince discovered the guard had abandoned his post, he would certainly be put to death. She didn't know if Wangshu was lying or really didn't know what happened to the guard. She supposed it didn't really matter at the moment.

"You can stay here for as long as you need," Lady Li said. "And don't worry, the inspector hasn't given up on finding the real killer yet."

"I am glad of it," Wangshu said, returning to her bowl of food. "I couldn't go back to the empress with this cloud of suspicion hanging over me. She has risked so much in putting me forward. What would people say if they found out she was harboring a suspected murderess?"

Lady Li nodded. She initially thought that Wangshu would be safer if she returned to the empress, but she made a good point. It could be dangerous for the empress's reputation and standing if she took Wangshu in and then the rumors of her being a killer got out.

"Can I go to the theater and watch you perform again?" Second Daughter asked. Her chin was in her hands and she was staring dreamily at Wangshu.

First Daughter elbowed her sister in the side. "Don't interrupt when the adults are speaking."

"It's quite all right," Wangshu said. "But I don't know if I can bring myself to go back there. There is supposed to be another performance in three days, but just the thought of going back there again..." She shuddered.

"Don't worry about that right now," Lady Li said. "Three days is a long time from now. Who knows. Inspector Gong might even—" She cut herself off, remembering that her daughters had no idea they had witnessed a murder. She wanted to keep them innocent for as long as possible, and even hearing about Wangshu being attacked was more than she wanted them to hear. "Just...never you mind," she finally said. "Girls, go with nanny and get ready for bed. I'll be there to kiss you shortly."

"Yes, Mama," they said in unison, but Second Daughter lingered, never taking her eyes off of Wangshu as she dragged her feet out the door.

"Your younger daughter has the spirit of a performer," Wangshu said. "I can see it in her eyes."

"She is the more outgoing of the two," Lady Li said. "She is never afraid to speak loudly or be the center of attention."

"If the empress has her way, your daughter could be a great actress when she is old enough," Wangshu said.

Lady Li shook her head. "You know that is not in the sticks for women like us. I'll have to start thinking about her marriage soon. Marriages for both of them, actually." She sighed and picked at her rice, her appetite suddenly gone.

"The empress is changing not just opera, but the world," Wangshu said. "Between the empress and the British queen, has there ever been a better time to be a woman?"

Lady Li scoffed. "You think just because women are sitting on thrones that life is any easier for us behind closed doors? That we have any opportunities outside of them?"

"You don't answer to a man," Wangshu said. "Why should your daughters? You have money. Status. Things could be different for them if you wanted it to be."

Lady Li was shocked into silence. She hadn't considered that there could be another path for her daughters in life. But what would that path even look like? She wouldn't have any idea where to find it. If her daughters didn't marry, what would they do? They couldn't go to school. Couldn't learn a trade or be apprentices. They would just stay home, embroidering and reading books. What kind of life was that?

She gave Wangshu a smile but did not engage in the discussion further. "I will go see if your room is ready," she said.

"Thank you, again," Wangshu said. "I did not return to the Forbidden City for fear of bringing dishonor upon the empress, but I may have brought it here instead."

"Of course not," Lady Li said. "I am happy to help you. And by helping you, I am helping the empress. Even if you don't return to the palace, if you are arrested for the crime it would bring the empress great shame. I cannot allow that."

"And you think you lack the ability to change your daughters' fortunes?" Wangshu asked. "If you believed in yourself as much as you believed in me, I think you could move mountains."

Lady Li felt her face go hot at the compliment. She rushed from the room before tears fell from her eyes.

14

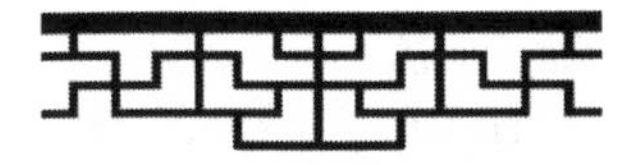

The next morning, Inspector Gong woke up and slipped out as soon as he heard the servants shuffling about so he could avoid his family. He also thought he would have a long day ahead of searching for Wangshu.

He couldn't simply ask Prince Kung if she had returned to the Forbidden City because then the prince would know he didn't know where she was. Even though it had been the prince and Lady Li who didn't let him arrest her in the first place. He should have at least locked her up somewhere, in an abandoned house or chicken coop or something. If he searched all day and still didn't find her, he would have to tell the prince.

He had told his men, men who helped him search for things or people or assisted him when he needed some extra muscle, to keep an eye out for her. Surprisingly, one of the men had news for him.

"A girl carrying some large bags was seen asking where Lady Li lived," the man told him.

He felt like a huge boulder had been lifted from his shoulders and he let out a loud exhale.

"Of course, she'd look for Lady Li," he said to himself. It seemed so obvious now. Lady Li had defended her, kept her from being arrested, and the two somewhat knew each other from Lady Li's years as a lady-in-waiting to the empress. He headed straight there.

A servant at Lady Li's mansion admitted him without having to ask for permission from Eunuch Bai or Lady Li. He was becoming a well-known visitor.

"Gong Shuhu!" First Daughter and Second Daughter cried, running toward him as soon as he entered the courtyard.

He smiled and picked up the girls, one in each arm, and spun them around before gently placing them back on their feet. He kneeled down to their level to talk to them.

"And what have you naughty monkeys been up to?"

"I'm going to be a great opera singer!" Second Daughter belted out dramatically. First Daughter only rolled her eyes.

Inspector Gong laughed. "And what made you decide this?"

"Wangshu has been telling me all about her life as an opera singer at the empress's court," Second Daughter explained, looking back to the table where she had been sitting with Wangshu and her mother, both of whom were now standing anxiously.

Inspector Gong stood and walked over to the two women. "So, this is where you decided to hide out until all this is over? Must be a great deal more comfortable than your little room at the theater."

"And safer," Lady Li added, her face expressionless and her hands folded in front of her.

"Oh?" he asked, raising an eyebrow.

"I was attacked," Wangshu said.

He nodded and stepped closer to them. "I think I need to hear more about this."

"Girls," Lady Li said, probably not wanting them to hear the troubling details. "It is time to visit with Popo."

"Yes, Mama," they said as they slinked away.

"Why don't you have a seat, inspector," Lady Li said.

He nodded, but before he could, Swan entered the courtyard.

"Oh!" she gasped, putting her hand to her mouth.

Inspector Gong stood and gave her a small bow, but then he locked eyes with her. She was...beautiful. More lovely than he had ever seen her before. Her face had color and her eyes appeared rested. She wore a simple gown and her hair was merely plaited down the back, but she seemed healthy. Youthful. Innocent.

"My Lady Swan," he said. "I am glad to see you are looking well."

She gave him a bow, as befitting a woman to her husband. "I am sorry to interrupt. I'll take my leave."

"No," the inspector said abruptly, surprising even himself. "Stay, please. We were about to discuss Wangshu's...unfortunate situation. You have helped me in the past. Perhaps you can offer some insight."

Her eyes sparkled and she kept her sleeve to her mouth as she smiled. "Yes, I'd love to."

He motioned for her to take a seat at the table, but as he did so, his eyes fell on Lady Li, and his own smile quavered. She was not looking at him, and she was neither smiling nor frowning. She wore only the impenetrable façade she had spent years practicing.

"Tea and cold dishes," Lady Li told a nearby servant, who bobbed her head and disappeared.

Inspector Gong, Wangshu, Lady Li, and Swan sat on their knees around the low table, enjoying the comfortable breeze in the shade of Lady Li's courtyard.

"I take it that Dr. Xue had been to see you, Lady Swan," Inspector Gong said.

"Yes," Swan said, keeping her eyes demurely downcast. "I can't remember the last time my mind felt so clear. And my appetite has returned. Thank you."

"I am glad to hear it," he said with a smile, but making a point not to look in Lady Li's direction. He was truly impressed with the progress Swan had made in such a short amount of time. Surely everyone was wrong about her not being a good choice as a wife. She only needed time to come out of the opium cloud. Of course, he would still prefer Lady Li, but Swan would be an acceptable alternative.

Two servants brought out a tray with a teapot, teacups, chopsticks, and several small plates of cold dishes such as pickled cucumbers in sauce, spicy lotus root, sautéed wood ear mushrooms, and almond cookies.

Inspector Gong used his chopsticks to grab a piece of cucumber while Swan, being the youngest person at the table, prepared the cups of tea.

"So, Wangshu, tell me about this attack in your dressing room," he said.

"It was terrible," she said, accepting a teacup from Swan. "He burst into the room, called me horrible names. He said I needed to be punished for daring to show myself publicly. I believe he was going to rape me." She shuddered.

Inspector Gong nodded slowly as he listened. "Go on," he said, and she did. The room did appear to be in disarray, but he couldn't say that an assault as she described had happened there. In fact, she mentioned every askew piece of furniture in her retelling of the events, which was oddly specific. He didn't want to voice his doubts, especially if she was telling the truth, but he had a feeling she wasn't being completely honest about what happened in her room.

"Can I trust you to stay here?" the inspector asked when she finished her story. "I need to know where you are at all times. I can't have you running away again."

"Yes, I'll stay here," Wangshu said. "Lady Li has been the most gracious host. I could not repay her by fleeing into the night."

"Of course, if someone would attack you in the theater, they could come for you here as well," the inspector said, and Wangshu blanched.

"What do you mean?" Lady Li asked.

"Wangshu is a subject of scorn," Inspector Gong asked. "Many people are not happy with her taking the place of a man, even if it is just on the stage. You know how people can work themselves up into a frenzy. What if they came here looking for her? I think I should station one of my men outside your gate at all times."

"How...*kind* of you," Wangshu said, but the inspector thought she meant anything but kind. Had she been planning on escaping again?

"Do you really think we could be in danger?" Swan asked.

"One can never be too careful," he said.

"Forget about that," Lady Li said, some irritation bubbling in her voice. "We need to find out who really killed Fanhua. Wangshu needs to get back to her life. There is supposed to be another opera performance in two days."

"I doubt that will happen," Inspector Gong said. "Changpu is furious that Wangshu left and took all the costumes with her."

"Most of those were *my* costumes," Wangshu said. "I brought them with me because the Dashu troupe was little more than a group of riverbed beggars."

"Changpu said the troupe dated back over a hundred years," the inspector said. "They performed for the Qianlong Emperor."

"That didn't keep his father or his grandfather from pilfering away their profits over the years," Wangshu said. "They had their name only. If the empress hadn't offered them such a substantial sum to take me on, they'd still be performing on the street."

The inspector wasn't sure what to make of this information just yet. Changpu had said he lived in a large house in an upscale district. He was hardly a riverbed beggar. Though he supposed it was possible Changpu had kept most of the money the troupe earned for himself while the other actors and theater employees starved. He had thought it was odd that so many people were living in the dressing rooms. Still, private squabbles between actors were not his concern. He only wondered if this had anything to do with Fanhua's murder.

"Changpu will probably make you prove you didn't steal them," the inspector said.

"My family will vouch for me," Wangshu said. "They never wanted me to do this. But...well, who can say no the empress?"

Everyone else nodded in commiseration. Even if they didn't know the empress personally, everyone knew her reputation—and she was not a woman you could easily deny when she set her mind to something.

"And what about you?" Lady Li asked Wangshu. "Did you want this assignment? This responsibility of being the first woman to perform opera in public?"

"Well, surely, Lady Li, you know I'm not the first woman to perform opera on stage," Wangshu said. "Only the first to do so with a woman's name."

"Wangshu?" the inspector asked. "That's not a very feminine name, is it? Is it your real name?"

Wangshu chuckled from behind her closed lips. "You are astute, Inspector Gong. No, Wangshu is not a traditional name for a woman, but it just...fit. It is a name I chose when I started performing for the empress."

"Wangshu is the god who drives the moon across the sky each night," Swan said in her soft voice. Inspector Gong gave her an appreciative smile.

"Quite," Wangshu said, nodding at Swan. "But in answer to your question, no, I didn't really want the responsibility. Like the empress, I thought that women who were already involved in opera outside the palace would be happy to start performing in their own right, but no one was willing. Someone had to do it, but I didn't want to leave my home, my family, all for what? Public scorn and humiliation?"

"For the future of opera," Lady Li said. "Thanks to you, more women will be able to perform now. It will just take time."

"Not if I lose my head over it!" Wangshu said. "It will be another hundred years before a woman tries a public performance if I'm executed for killing Fanhua."

"That won't happen," Inspector Gong said with more conviction than he possessed. "Just keep telling me what you know about Fanhua, Changpu, the theater, that night. Everything. I will find the person behind this." Whether he would find the real killer before or after Wangshu was held responsible for Fanhua's death was another matter.

"I'm doing my best, inspector," Wangshu said.

Inspector Gong doubted that, but he pressed ahead anyway.

"Tell me about your relationship with Fanhua," the inspector said as he sipped his tea, not taking his eyes off of Wangshu.

"I'm not sure what there is to tell," she said looking pensively at her teacup. "We were...friendly, but he was greatly distraught over the loss of his role as the dan. But we were making the best of it."

"In what way?" the inspector asked.

"We spent time together," Wangshu said. "He showed me how he played the role of Xueyan and we worked together to help me improve on it. He supported me being on the stage, even if it meant he lost the role. It wasn't as though he had to leave the theater. He was still able to play the wusheng. And if he really had his heart set on playing the dan, he could have gone to another troupe, or just started his own."

"Would it be that easy?" Inspector Gong asked. "To just move to a new troupe?"

"Not always," Wangshu said. "But for someone as talented and popular as Fanhua, other troupes would be climbing the gates to have him."

There was something in her tone that he couldn't quite identify. Something she was hinting at or leading him toward.

"Were you and Fanhua..." Swan started, but then hesitated. She looked to Inspector Gong, and he nodded, urging her on. She smiled and sat up a little straighter. "Were you having an affair?"

Wangshu's smile quavered, just a bit, so slightly it was hardly noticeable. She looked down and her head swayed from side to side. She held her hand to her mouth and let out a giggle. Her movements were so practiced, so precise, it was as though she was performing an opera right in front of them, and Inspector Gong knew she was going to lie to them.

"Well, not yet," Wangshu said. "But it was certainly headed in that direction."

Inspector Gong suppressed the urge to call her out for her lie right there. He had too many sources telling him that Fanhua was only interested in men to discount them. The question was why Wangshu would lie about her relationship with Fanhua. The only thing he knew for certain was that Wangshu, for whatever reason, couldn't be trusted.

"If it wasn't you," the inspector said, doing his best to mask his annoyance, but he was far from a skilled opera performer, "who wanted Fanhua dead, then who? I haven't found a single person with a motive to take the poor boy out."

"I think the problem," Lady Li said, leaning over to refill Inspector Gong's teacup, "is that your investigation isn't focused. You are dividing your attention on both who wanted Fanhua dead and who would want to frame Wangshu. Am I correct?"

Inspector Gong thought about his interviews so far and realized she was right. While he would start talking to people about Wangshu, the conversation would eventually drift to Fanhua.

"That might be a fair assumption," he said.

"The question is, who is the real victim?" Lady Li said. "Was someone trying to kill Fanhua and used Wangshu as the weapon? Or was that person trying to frame Wangshu and Fanhua was merely collateral damage?"

"If someone wanted to kill Fanhua," Swan interjected, "they could have done it any other time or place. They could have done it more...secretly. Not on stage for everyone to see."

"It was no coincidence the murder happened my first night on stage," Wangshu added.

"And we cannot forget that the murder weapon was the sword, the prop that was switched," Lady Li said.

"So the killer must be someone at the theater," Swan said, excitement causing her cheeks to flush.

Inspector Gong chuckled as he watched the three ladies discuss the crime. They were clever enough that if left to their own devices, they would probably solve the murder on their own. He couldn't let that happen.

"I agree," he interjected. "I believe that Wangshu was the intended victim of this crime, so that is where I need to focus my investigation. I should be going. I have many more people to speak to."

He stood, as did all three of the ladies. He bowed to each of them, but he let his eyes linger for a moment on Swan, which was completely inappropriate since she was to be his betrothed. But he was impressed with her contributions to his questioning of Wangshu. She was a very clever girl, someone he could talk to, if they ever had a moment alone. Everything else about their courtship had been unconventional. Perhaps Lady Li would let him call on Swan...

He shook his head and looked away. He couldn't do that to Lady Li, ask for permission to call on Swan in her home. He and Lady Li had already been together intimately in that same home. Did Swan know about that?

Suddenly he felt uncomfortable with all of the women's eyes on him. He offered one last bow and then excused himself, but Lady Li escorted him out.

"Are you all right?" she asked him at the gate.

He wasn't. He felt confused. Conflicted. And as he looked at Lady Li, the feelings only got worse.

"I'm fine," he said. "But keep an eye on Wangshu. She wasn't telling the whole truth back there. I don't know why she's lying to me, to you, but she is."

Lady Li pressed her lips and nodded. "I will. And I'll let you know if I learn anything else."

They looked at each other, unsure of what else to say. He wanted to hold her, tell her he was sorry for looking at Swan. The guilt was washing over him, burying him. He couldn't take it. He needed to focus.

Without a goodbye, he opened the gate and stormed out into the street.

15

Inspector Gong went back to the White Lotus Theater. The line of thinking that the killer was someone associated with the theater was a good one. Someone must have been familiar with the play and the prop sword and be familiar enough to the members of the troupe that no one would have found the killer suspicious.

As he entered the theater, he noticed that there was no guard to keep people out. As he thought about it, he realized that didn't remember ever seeing a guard. It had been the prince's men who ushered the crowd out and kept them outside on the night of Fanhua's murder. On the night of the show, after Wangshu killed Fanhua, he had been able to simply walk backstage with no one trying to stop him. No one kept Lady Li or Prince Kung from going backstage either. At the time, he had chalked it up to the fact that he and Prince Kung were well-known, so no one would stop them from going wherever they wanted to go. But now, he wondered if the theater ever had a guard at all, someone to keep the crowds and the admirers at bay. If not, then anyone could have snuck in and changed the sword. Still, it would have to have been someone who wouldn't have drawn attention and would know where the prop sword had been kept.

On the stage, five women were performing one of Xueyan's dances from *The Concubine's Lover* under Changpu's watchful eye. None of them were as graceful as Wangshu had been, though. Inspector Gong marveled at the fact that he knew that. One night at the theater and suddenly he was an opera expert. Changpu must have been holding auditions for new actresses to join the troupe. It wasn't until he got right up to the edge of the stage and looked at the performers more closely that he realized they were actually men. Young, thin, effeminate men like Fanhua had been.

"No! No! No!" Changpu exclaimed, throwing up his hands. "Slower. With more grace. Have any of you ever actually *seen* a woman?"

The men tried to follow Changpu's direction but were now clearly flustered as they missed their cues or faltered on their tall pot-bottom shoes.

That's enough," Changpu finally said. "Leave. I'll let you know if I decide to settle for any of you."

The actors grumbled as they left the stage in a huff.

"Holding auditions for a new dan?" Inspector Gong asked as he ascended the stage.

"Torturing myself is more like it," Changpu said, shaking his head. "These boys think they can just put on a dress and be a dan. They don't seem to understand how to embody the essence of a woman."

"Why are you not auditioning women for the role?" the inspector asked. "You said you were comfortable with Wangshu being a member of the troupe."

Changpu grimaced and then nodded. "Well, given the outcome of that little experiment, surely you can understand my hesitance to take on another woman so soon. Maybe someday…" He let his voice trail off, apparently not seeing the need to further justify his decision.

Inspector Gong couldn't blame him. What Changpu undoubtedly thought would be a quick way to earn some money and the good graces of the empress had cost him his dan, his wusheng, and had brought him untold negative attention. And most people didn't even know about the murder yet.

"I don't know how we are going to be ready for the performance in only two days," Changpu lamented. "Even if I do find a new dan, I'm not sure how he will learn the role so quickly."

"Can you hire someone who already knows the role?" the inspector asked. "How popular is *The Concubine's Lover*?"

"It is a rather well-known opera," Changpu said. "Many of our regular patrons saw Fanhua perform in it dozens of times. It is a show that should be in any troupe's repertoire."

"So it would be common knowledge that a sword is used to kill the general toward the end of the show," the inspector said, more to himself than to Changpu, but Changpu nodded.

"Tell me," the inspector went on as he surveyed the stage and saw a crate of props sitting off to one side. "I noticed you didn't have a guard to protect the actors or keep people from going backstage. How do you protect yourselves or keep things orderly?"

Changpu stuck out his chin. "We never needed any sort of protection before Wangshu joined the troupe. People who attend the theater know the rules. They respect tradition and the…the mystery of it all. If they were to see Fanhua out of costume, the magic of it all would be lost."

"I understand that," the inspector said. "But that means anyone could go backstage or simply be here in the theater at any time without reason. On the night of the murder, did you see anyone messing with the props who shouldn't have?"

Changpu laughed. "So you believe her little story about some phantom switching out the swords?"

"I'm pursuing several angles," the inspector replied. "And it makes no sense for her to murder someone in cold blood in front of an audience. But I take it you believe differently?"

"What I believe," Changpu said, "is that Wangshu is the most gifted actress I have ever seen. I don't know why she would want to kill Fanhua, but I would not be so quick to assume she didn't have her reasons."

"Well, if you discover her reason, do let me know," Inspector Gong said. "But until then, I'll be looking for whoever switched that sword."

Changpu sighed. "I don't remember seeing anyone, but Fanhua frequently let his little admirers visit him backstage. There was always some simpering female mooning about."

Inspector Gong thought about what Hungjian had insisted. That since Fanhua was a cut sleeve, he didn't entertain female lovers. What Changpu said seemed to contradict that.

"I hope you find the killer soon," Changpu went on. "It's too late to cancel the next show, and tickets have sold out. I might be able to find a new wusheng, but I need Wangshu to play the dan one more time. After that, I can close the theater until I find someone new or stage a play without a female role."

"Who will you get to play the role of the wusheng?" the inspector asked.

"Hungjian, the face-changer," Changpu said.

"Isn't he popular enough already?" the inspector asked. "And Szechuan opera is a completely different style. How can he just step into the role of the wusheng?"

"Assuming a new role in an instant is what Hungjian does," Changpu said. "Though you are right about him being popular. I assume he wants to amass Fanhua's admirers for himself. By combining Fanhua's following with his own, why any troupe in the city would be clamoring for Hungjian to join them. Now, if you'll excuse me."

Inspector Gong let Changpu leave the stage. He wondered if Hungjian could be the killer after all. Maybe he always planned to take Fanhua's place, garner his followers for himself.

Inspector Gong then realized that he once again had faltered in his original line of inquisition. Instead of focusing on who was framing Wangshu, he had ended up trying to figure out who would want to eliminate Fanhua. The women had made it sound like following one line of questioning was so easy, but it was all connected somehow, he was sure of it. Fanhua was simply too popular to be "collateral damage," as Lady Li had called him. Fanhua was too high of a cost to get rid of Wangshu. No one would have simply killed the boy without cause. It was too risky. Too conspicuous. Besides, with the backstage completely accessible, anyone could have killed Wangshu at any time. Or Fanhua for that matter.

Someone must have been sending a message. Inspector Gong simply needed to decipher it. Was the killer sending a message to Wangshu? A threat? A warning? A message that she should not try to take the place of a man. Possibly.

Was the message for Changpu? Telling him he should not allow a woman to perform in his troupe? Again, possibly, but he felt that was unlikely. Changpu had only been doing as ordered by the empress.

Was the message for the empress? That was certainly a possibility. A warning to her to not upset the status quo.

He supposed the message could have been for Fanhua, who certainly got the point of it. But why make a public display of it? Why attract the attention? If the message had been for Fanhua, it must not have been *only* for Fanhua, but for the theater community at large.

But what was the message? What was the killer trying to say by killing the opera scene's most popular actor?

Unfortunately, Inspector Gong didn't know the theater world well enough to understand the message on his own. He would have to keep looking, keep inquiring, keep digging.

16

Lady Li felt energized after her conversation about the case with Inspector Gong, Swan, and Wangshu. She was irritated by the way Inspector Gong had deferred to Swan and gave her so much attention, but that was overshadowed by the fact that there might be some progress on finding Fanhua's killer. Mostly. She wavered back and forth between feeling slighted by Inspector Gong and accepting that things were progressing the way they should. If Inspector Gong was going to marry Swan, then he should show her the most attention. In truth, he shouldn't be showing Lady Li any attention at all. He shouldn't be in her home and he shouldn't be relying on her to help him solve his latest case.

Actually, he wasn't relying on her. He hadn't asked for her assistance at all this time like he had in the past. He was only investigating because she and the prince had asked him to. Any information she had gleaned about the case had come from her own investigating, and she wasn't sure she had learned anything useful.

"I'm going out," she declared to Wangshu and Swan, who looked at her with surprise.

"Where are you going?" Wangshu asked.

"To speak with one of Fanhua's admirers," Lady Li admitted. "They knew Fanhua better than anyone perhaps, so they might know something no one else would know. One of them might even have killed him."

"Killed someone they profess to love?" Swan asked, aghast.

"Love is a powerful force," Wangshu said knowingly. "Many operas use love as a driving force behind murder as the plot."

"I suppose that's true," Swan said. "Same with novels. But I suppose I never thought of people actually killing those they loved in real life. It's too awful to imagine."

"I agree it is a very wicked thing to happen," Lady Li said. "But it is an all too real possibility. And Inspector Gong can't talk to the young women who followed Fanhua on his own, so I must call on them."

"Did he ask you for your help?" Swan asked, standing up.

"Of course, he did," Lady Li lied. "I wouldn't do something so reckless on my own."

Swan sighed dreamily. "I hope to be as useful to him one day as you are."

"You just focus on getting well," Lady Li said. "Have a rest. Drink the tea Dr. Xue left for you."

Swan gave Lady Li a small bow. "Yes, my lady," she said and solemnly headed to her room.

"The inspector didn't really ask for your help, did he?" Wangshu asked the moment Swan was out of earshot.

Lady Li felt her ears go hot. "What do you mean?" she asked innocently, but knew she'd been caught.

"Don't try to lie to me," Wangshu said. "I lie...I mean, *act* for a living."

"I suppose acting is a form of deceit, isn't it?" Lady Li said. "Perhaps that is why so many people think it is a rather unsuitable job for a woman—"

"Don't try to change the subject," Wangshu interrupted. "Why are you doing this if the inspector didn't ask you to? Do you know something he doesn't?"

Lady Li chuckled. "Oh, I know a great deal he doesn't."

Wangshu cocked her eyebrow suggestively.

"I didn't mean..." Lady Li started to say but let her words wonder off. Of course, she had meant it in the way Wangshu understood it, she had never had anyone around who understood her double entendres before. "I just mean that Inspector Gong often needs more assistance with his cases than he realizes. He prefers to work alone, but he doesn't know everything."

"You seem to know this man who isn't related to you quite well," Wangshu said. Lady Li opened her mouth as though scandalized, but then Wangshu said, "Well done."

"W-w-why?" Lady Li couldn't help but ask in surprise.

"I live in a world that would make most people blush," Wangshu said. "A world where women work as writers and poets and men have scandalous affairs with other men. Humans are complicated creatures who find happiness in many ways in life, not only the ways our grandparents wish we should stick to."

Lady Li finally resigned herself to the fact that this girl, this opera performer, understood her far better than anyone else. While she still couldn't admit to her relationship with Inspector Gong, she could perhaps unburden herself a tiny bit.

"I'm only twenty-five years old," Lady Li said. "The

world would have me spend the rest of my life as a widow. The very thought makes me miserable. Yet I can't seem to bring myself to rebel. I don't know another way to live, and I can't imagine what such action would do to my daughters and their future.

"The same is true of Swan," she went on. "She should remain a widow as well even though she is only twenty, barely older than a girl. But I have found a way for her to escape this life and I think she needs to take it."

"Even at your own cost?" Wangshu asked. Lady Li did not look at her or respond. "The desire that pours off of you when you look at the inspector is infectious. And the lust in his eyes for you..." She sighed and fanned herself with her hand. "We should all hope to find a man who looks at us like that. But you are willing to give him up for her? Why?"

"I can't stand in the way of her happiness, of her freedom," Lady Li said. "I'm frustrated. Jealous. Sad, even. But I love her as a sister. At least, I think I do. I didn't have one growing up. Sisters fight, don't they? If I can help her escape this life, I will do it."

Wangshu shook her head in disbelief and amazement. "You are a goddess among women, Lady Li," she said. "Daughters and widows will be forced to write poems about your piety and light incense in your name for generations to come."

Lady Li paused at that. Where had she heard it before? Was that really all her future held for her? Misery in this life and forced misery upon girls who had yet to be born? She certainly wasn't doing this to be honored. She was not an example to be imitated.

Finding neither comfort nor reassurance in Wangshu's words, Lady Li stood to leave. "I should go make my call before it is too late."

"Let me know what you discover," Wangshu said.

Lady Li arrived at Liling's house to find it in a tizzy. The maid who admitted her seemed frazzled, as though unsure of what to do, while the other household staff moved about quickly and quietly. There was shouting and crying from the back of the house, so Lady Li headed in that direction.

"Liling!" a woman was yelling. "You must calm yourself."

"He's dead!" Liling cried. "What am I going to do?"

"He's just an opera singer," the woman whom Lady Li assumed was Liling's mother said. "There are others."

"No!" Liling yelled. "There will never be another."

"Who died?" Lady Li asked, though she had a feeling she knew exactly who had Liling upset.

Lining's mother looked at Lady Li in shock. "Who are you? Who admitted you?"

"I'm...a friend of Liling's," Lady Li said with a smile. "We met at the opera and I was calling to talk to her about Wangshu's performance—"

"Don't speak to me of that bitch!" Liling railed at Lady Li.

"Liling!" her mother gasped. "What has gotten into you?"

"Could you just give us a moment," Lady Li said to Liling's mother. "I'm sure I can help if I talk to her."

"Good luck," her mother scoffed. "She's been like this all morning!" She shook her head and tottered away.

"Now, Liling," Lady Li said, entering the girl's room and closing the door. "What happened? Why are you so upset?"

"It's Fanhua!" she wailed, plopping down on her bed. "He's dead!"

"What?" Lady Li gasped in surprise, sitting down beside her. "How? Who told you?"

"Everyone is talking about it," Liling said, wiping her nose on her sleeve and handing Lady Li a small two-page newspaper. "A friend sent this over."

On the front page of the paper was a story announcing the death of Fanhua. It didn't have the details, but it did mention that Wangshu was missing and made it sound like she was somehow involved in Fanhua's death. Other than that, the report had no information about the death but talked about Fanhua's short but illustrious career. At first, Lady Li wondered why she hadn't heard this since she read the papers, but she quickly realized that she didn't subscribe to this one. It seemed to be dedicated to entertainment news around the city, including not only opera performances, but British and Japanese theater news as well. It wasn't something most respectable ladies would subscribe to, but Lady Li was sure it had a large underground support network. She had no idea who would have leaked the news about Fanhua's death, but it didn't seem to matter now. Surely by now all the opera patrons in town would know about it.

"Oh, Liling," Lady Li said, patting her on the back. "I am so sorry. I know how important he was to you."

"This is the worst thing to ever happen in my life,"

Liling said, standing up and pacing, and Lady Li thought the poor girl—as sheltered as she was—probably wasn't exaggerating. "How could this happen?"

"Tragedies happen, my dear," Lady Li said. "Sometimes for no reason at all."

"This is all Wangshu's fault," Liling spat. "How could she do this?"

"What do you mean?" Lady Li prodded. Did Liling somehow know something about Fanhua's death?

"She stole his role," Liling said. "Forced him to play a man. You think it is a coincidence that he died after suffering such humiliation? I saw him before the show, in his general costume. He was so distraught! He smashed the mirror on his dresser. He hated what he saw."

"But...he was a man," Lady Li said. "How could it be a humiliation to play one on stage?"

Liling scoffed. "You really are new to the opera world, aren't you?"

Lady Li held out her hands helplessly.

"He wasn't supposed to play a man," Liling said. "He... how can I explain this? My own mother doesn't even understand me when I talk about it."

"Do try," Lady Li said. "I want to know what made him so appealing. I was never fortunate enough to see him in the role of the dan."

Liling seemed to seize upon the opportunity to share her love of Fanhua and the opera with someone new. She sat back down next to Lady Li and squeezed her hand. "Have you ever wanted to be a man?" she asked. "Maybe not...physically. But wished to have their freedom? To go where you want and do what you want with no barriers?"

Lady Li chuckled. "Who hasn't?"

Liling nodded. "Fanhua was what we all wanted to be. A

woman with the freedom of a man. But for him to...to no longer be one of us—to be a wusheng—what's the point of that? A man playing a man. How novel," she said sarcastically.

"But what about Wangshu?" Lady Li asked. "Isn't having a woman play a woman—going where women have never been allowed before—isn't that better than a man pretending to be a woman. A man *acting* like he understands our struggles when in truth the world is an open door to him?"

"Wangshu isn't free," Liling said. "She's just a slave to the empress. She still must answer to a man—her troupe leader, her father, eventually her husband."

Lady Li wanted to argue more, but she didn't think that would be a good way to get Liling to open up to her. So she bit her tongue and smiled.

"I see," Lady Li said, even though she was still confused.

"To think my dear Fanhua died after his final role was that of a man," Liling said sadly. "How his soul must have ached to meet his ancestors dressed like that. Wangshu stole his last performance from him. She should forever be punished for that."

"Do you think that one of Fanhua's admirers could have hurt him?" Lady Li dared to ask. She was tiring of dealing with such an emotional child. Would her own daughters be this dramatic when they got older? She certainly hoped not.

"Is that what you think?" Liling asked, her eyes wide. "That someone might have killed Fanhua?"

"I don't know," Lady Li said, looking back at the thin newspaper. "The article didn't say. But he was young and healthy, wasn't he? What do you think happened to him?"

"But...we love him," Liling said. "No one would dare hurt Fanhua. We would do anything to protect him."

"And Wangshu?" Lady Li asked. "What about her?"

Liling's eyes went dark and she pinched her lips together before speaking. "I'm glad she's gone. Maybe she is dead too."

Lady Li nodded and then stood to leave. "Again, I am so sorry for your loss." She left Liling's room without any other pleasantries and didn't bother excusing herself to Liling's mother. She had no plans on seeing these people ever again anyway.

As she rode back home, she wasn't sure she learned anything new that would help the case, but more than ever, she doubted any of Fanhua's admirers would have done anything to cause him harm. But they seemed to hate Wangshu with as much passion as they loved Fanhua. If love was a motivator to commit murder, hate certainly was as well. Could someone have been so blinded by their hate of Wangshu that Fanhua simply got in the way of someone trying to take her out? Lady Li supposed it was possible, if not terribly realistic.

She hated the idea of not having anything to offer Inspector Gong with relation to the case when she saw him again. Even though she shouldn't be trying to get his attention, she already missed feeling useful to him. There had to be something she could do to help.

She ordered her chair-bearers to take her to the theater. Perhaps she would find a clue there that he had overlooked.

17

Inspector Gong doubted it was a coincidence that Hungjian was going to be taking Fanhua's place in the troupe, so he went back to the Green Willow Theater to speak with him some more.

When he walked into the theater, he saw a man comforting two crying women. He didn't recognize the man, so he skirted around them as he headed backstage.

"But what if something happens to you?" he heard one of the women ask.

"I can't live without you," the other one said.

They must have learned about Fanhua's death. He wasn't surprised. Someone from the audience could have realized what happened. Fanhua also now hadn't been seen for days. There were also many people who worked at the White Lotus Theater who could have let the news slip. The news of the boy's death undoubtedly had spread through the opera community like wildfire once it was out.

Inspector Gong tried to slip past the actor and his admirers when he heard a familiar voice.

"Don't worry, my pets," the man said. "No one could

dare hurt me. They'd have to find me first." The girls giggled.

Inspector Gong turned back and realized that the man was Hungjian, but his face looked completely different even though he wasn't wearing a mask.

"Hungjian," the inspector said. "We need to talk."

The women huddled more closely to Hungjian.

"Now?" Hungjian asked. "Can't you see I'm a little busy."

"Now," the inspector said, motioning backstage.

Hungjian sighed. "Forgive me, my dears," he said. "But I cannot keep the inspector waiting."

"Inspector?" one of the girls asked in between hiccups. "Are you going to find out who killed Fanhua?"

"I am sure I will," the inspector said.

"It was probably that dreadful woman," the other girl said without having to say Wangshu's name.

The inspector rolled his eyes. "So I've heard."

"Who else could it be?" the first girl asked, not really wanting an answer. "A woman with no morals, displaying herself like that in front of men. There is no telling how far her depravity goes."

"Do your mothers know you are out in public?" the inspector asked.

The girls' mouths gaped in shock, but they knew they didn't have a retort. It was rather cheeky for women who snuck out of their homes to meet an actor would criticize another woman for acting improperly.

"Head home, girls," Hungjian said. "I'll see you for the performance tonight."

The girls nodded as their eyes welled up again, but they turned away to exit the theater.

Inspector Gong examined Hungjian's face as they walked back to Hungjian's dressing room, trying to figure out why he looked so different. His cheekbones were more pronounced and his nose appeared longer. His eyebrows were more arched and his lips looked thinner. He finally realized that Hungjian had used a bit of makeup to adjust his features.

Hungjian noticed the inspector staring at him and gave a wink. "See something you like?"

"I'm just wondering which face is the real Hungjian," the inspector said as they entered the dressing room.

Hungjian sat at his dressing table and checked his appearance. He chuckled. "Oh, many people have tried to find the answer to that. But I am afraid they are still looking."

"You don't want to play games with me, Hungjian," the inspector said. "If I tell the Ministry of Justice you killed Fanhua, they will believe me."

Hungjian froze, his perfectly painted lips pursed tightly. He gave a hard look at the inspector. "You would point the finger at an innocent man?"

"I don't know if you are innocent," the inspector said as he glanced around the room at the various costumes and masks. "But I don't think you've been honest with me, so you must be hiding something."

"We all have secrets, inspector," Hungjian said. "Even you. That doesn't mean I would kill my...my friend."

"Even to get his spot in his opera troupe," the inspector asked. "For a chance to gain his admirers for yourself?"

"That's..." Hungjian started to yell, jumping up from the table, but then he paused to collect himself. "That's just business. What happened to Fanhua is a tragedy, but... what can I do about it? Changpu needs a new wusheng and it's a good opportunity for me. Should I just not take the role?"

For the opportunity to be pure business, Hungjian sure took the implications personally, the inspector thought.

"I can't tell you what to do," the inspector said, "only what I observe."

"And what are you observing right now?" Hungjian asked, crossing his arms, as though daring the inspector to make some sort of formal accusation.

Inspector Gong let out a long exhale, as though the accusation of murder meant nothing to him as he continued to look around the room. Finally, his eyes fell on a familiar bit of cloth, a cloak that appeared hastily hidden under several other costumes but the scalloped edge of which was still visible.

The inspector walked over to the pile of costumes and pulled the cloak free. "I observe that Fanhua may have been more than just a friend to you," he said.

Hungjian's face fell. Then his shoulders slumped a bit. He knew he had been caught. He stepped over and shut the door, even though the room was sweltering without any other ventilation.

"Fine," Hungjian said, facing the inspector. "I admit it. Fanhua...we were lovers."

"Why not tell me when you first told me that Fanhua was attracted to men? Inspector Gong asked. "You said it was common for theater actors to be that way."

"I said it was common for dan actors to be cut sleeves," Hungjian said. "Not a face changer like me. Not for men who play more masculine roles."

"So it was an open secret that Fanhua was attracted to men," the inspector said. "But a closed one for you?"

"Something like that," Hungjian said as he took the cloak from the inspector and ran the silk through his fingers.

"Something like what?" the inspector insisted. "I told you, this is no time to keep hiding from me. If you want Fanhua's killer found, I need the truth."

"I don't know who killed him," Hungjian said. "But it wasn't me. I loved him. We loved each other. But we couldn't live openly. We both had our admirers for different reasons. His loved him for his femininity, but they still expected him to be a man in the ways that count. Mine love me as a full man in every way. We couldn't..." He sighed and shook his head in exasperation. "If we wanted to remain popular with the patrons, we had to fulfill our roles—on stage and off."

"Sounds exhausting," Inspector Gong said.

"You have no idea," Hungjian said. "But a career in the theater doesn't last long. It's physically very demanding. And as you get older, well, the young women won't want to waste their affection or their money on someone fat with gray hair. We hoped to earn as much money as possible over the years and one day retire somewhere private."

Inspector Gong had some idea of what it was like to love someone secretly while having no hope of being together, but he kept his face expressionless.

"You said that the women expected Fanhua to be a man 'in the ways that count.' What did you mean exactly?" Inspector Gong asked. "Was he having affairs with some of his admirers? How did that make you feel?"

Hungjian looked away as though ashamed. "We both would spend time outside the theater with certain patrons... for a price."

"You were both prostituting yourselves?" the inspector asked.

"You don't have to make it sounds so dirty," Hungjian said. "It's an easy way to make a lot of money."

"Don't you make enough money from your performances?" the inspector asked.

"Please," Hungjian scoffed. "Our troupe leaders pay us only a pittance. A fraction of what we bring in for the troupe as a whole."

"Maybe one of Fanhua's patrons arranged his death," the inspector said. "A jilted lover? Someone who found out he preferred men?"

"We were very careful about keeping the truth secret," Hungjian said.

"I doubt that," the inspector said. "The other members of Fanhua's troupe knew he preferred men."

"Well, when you live and work so closely with other people, it can be hard to keep anything a secret for long," Hungjian said. "But the girls know what they are paying for. Just a night. Just a performance. A fantasy."

"Still, I think it is an avenue worth pursuing," Inspector Gong said. "Did Fanhua have any regular patrons? And I mean patrons who paid for sex, not just for the opera performance."

"There were a few," Hungjian said. "A girl named Jingzhu was one. Baoah was another. Liling. Hualing—"

"Any family names for these girls?" Inspector Gong interrupted. "Or where they lived?"

"I wasn't involved in that aspect of Fanhua's life," Hungjian said quickly.

Inspector Gong understood that, if Hungjian was as in love with Fanhua as he said. Though he couldn't help but have his doubts. It was a good story. One that made sense. Yet Hungjian lied and told stories for a living. Hungjian could just be putting on another mask. But he would take Hungjian at his word for now and see if any of his leads panned out.

"I suppose Fanhua must have kept some sort of record of his liaisons," Inspector Gong said. "Do you know where he would have kept the money he was saving?"

"I do, actually," Hungjian said. "In his dressing room, in the back west corner is a loose board. There's a tin box under it. The money should be there."

"You know where it is but haven't taken it for yourself?" the inspector asked, surprised.

"It honestly hadn't occurred to me until just now," Hungjian replied with a defeated sigh.

"I suppose you think I should give the money to you if it is still there," Inspector Gong said.

Hungjian scoffed. "If I say yes, I look like a money grubbing whore. If I say no, I'm a fool. What answer should I give you?"

Inspector Gong moved to open the door. "Just tell me the truth," the inspector said. "And when this is over, maybe I'll deem you worthy of the money."

The side of Hunjian's mouth cocked in a half-smile. "Life is cruel, isn't it?" he said. "But I think you might know a little something about that."

"We all have our demons," the inspector admitted as he showed himself out.

He went back to the White Lotus Theater to check Fanhua's dressing room for the money and any records of who his other lovers might have been.

The crowd of mourners—mostly young women—outside the theater had grown exponentially. They were all wailing and hugging each other. The other actors in the troupe, Kangjun, Laquan, and Pingru, were acting as guards to the front gate to keep the women from getting inside.

"I see Changpu finally decided to hire some security,"

Inspector Gong said after forcing his way through the crowd.

"Hire?" Kangju asked. "We were just told to keep the yowling cats out. They were trying to get backstage to his room and steal whatever they could. Bits of costumes and jewelry."

"They all want a piece of him, even now," Laquan said, an air of disgust on his tongue.

"I'll send for my own men to come and relieve you once I'm done looking through Fanhua's room myself," the inspector said as he went through the gate. He hoped the women hadn't stolen anything of importance.

When he opened the door to Fanhua's dressing room, he was surprised to hear someone gasp. Lady Li was already there.

"What are you doing here?" she asked.

"*I'm* investigating a murder," he said, closing the door behind him. "What are you doing here?"

"Oh," she said, as though she just realized that she shouldn't be here. "I just thought another perspective might help. That I might see something here you missed before."

He ran his hand over his mouth to hide a smile. In the past, she had only helped with his investigations because she didn't have much of a choice. He needed her. But now that he hadn't asked for her assistance, she couldn't stand being left out. The question was whether she was here because she was invested in the case or if she just wanted to spend time with him. He hoped it was the latter but knew it was probably the former. She was truly concerned for Wangshu's welfare after all.

"And have you?" he asked, taking a step closer toward her in the small room.

"H-have I what?" she asked.

"Found anything?" he asked, moving over toward the dressing table and wiped some of the glass shards from the smashed mirror away from some papers.

"Oh," she said with a gulp. "No. I haven't been here long."

"I wonder what happened in here," he said. "Who broke the mirror."

"One of Fanhua's admirers, a girl named Liling," Lady Li said, "told me that Fanhua smashed the mirror when he saw himself in the general costume. That he hated the masculine face looking back at him."

Inspector Gong remembered that Liling was one of the names Hungjian had mentioned as being one of Fanhua's patrons. "Liling was backstage the night of the murder?" Inspector Gong asked. "She told you this?"

"Yes," Lady Li said, and then her eyes widened. "She could have switched the swords!"

"Exactly," Inspector Gong said, moving toward the door to go question the girl himself. "Where does she live?"

"No, wait," Lady Li said. "She only just found out about Fanhua's death today. I was there not long after she learned the news. She was devastated. Out of her mind with grief."

"She could have just been pretending," Inspector Gong said. "Putting on a show of sorrow for you."

"I don't think so," Lady Li said. "I didn't make an appointment to call on her. And she was already railing at her mother before she knew I was there. I don't think it was an act."

"I'll take your word at it for now," he said. "But if we find more evidence..." His voice trailed off. He didn't like postponing questioning the girl, but if she were from a wealthy family, he would need strong evidence in order to even speak with her, much less arrest her.

He started pulling papers out of the drawers of the dressing table. They looked like pages from scripts. "What do you make of all this?" he asked Lady Li as she went over to the costumes and started going through the pockets. "Of these young ladies being obsessed with a man who appears as a woman?"

"I can't hardly credit it," Lady Li replied. "I find no appeal in such a man."

Inspector Gong couldn't help but smile to himself. "What sort of man appeals to you?"

Lady Li didn't reply, but he could almost feel the heat of her blush from across the room. Finally, she cleared her throat.

"Actually, while I was in the Forbidden City, I know there were women who...found solace in the arms of other women," she said. "The emperor could not spend enough time with all his wives and concubines. And there were many maids who also live in near captivity in the palace. But those relationships were women with other women. I don't understand the appeal of a man who appears as a woman. But to each their own I suppose. I can't understand how the empress—" She cut herself off.

"How the empress...?" Inspector Gong prompted.

"Never mind," Lady Li said. "We shouldn't speak of such things."

Now the inspector was intrigued. What did she know about the empress she couldn't tell him? He knew she would give her all to protect her friend, so if she didn't want to tell him there was no point in pressuring her.

"Are you looking for anything specific?" she asked him.

"Letters from patrons. Admirers," the inspector said. "The women who were his lovers. According to Hungjian, Fanhua had regular clients who paid for his affections."

"He was prostituting himself?" Lady Li asked, her eyes wide.

"To put it bluntly," Inspector Gong said. "Why? Do you know something about it?"

"I've spoken to some of the young ladies who regularly attended his performances," she said. "Liling, Baoah. But I didn't think..."

"Didn't think what?" he pushed.

"The girls are from good families," Lady Li said. "They are a bit neglected, just being daughters in large families. It's how they are able to get away with sneaking away to operas. But that they would...pay for a man to...I just can't imagine. If anyone found out, they would be ruined!"

Inspector Gong knew what she meant. If it were revealed that a young lady was having an affair with a man—opera singer or not—her reputation would be tarnished beyond repair. She could never make a favorable marriage match. Not to mention the damage to her family. It could ruin marriage prospects for her siblings as well. It could cost her father important connections. It was a ridiculous risk the young girls were taking in associating with Fanhua, much less with actually sleeping with him.

"If one of the women thought that Fanhua might reveal their affair..." said Inspector Gong.

"It could be enough reason for any one of them to kill him," Lady Li finished.

Inspector Gong went to the door, opening it to make sure no one was around. He then shut the door firmly and went to the west corner of the room. He tapped the floor with his foot, looking for the loose board.

"What are you doing?" Lady Li asked.

"Hungjian said that Fanhua kept his savings in a tin

under the floor," he explained. "Maybe he kept records of his liaisons there too."

One of the boards creaked. He kneeled down and lifted it up. Just where Hungjian had said it would be, he found a tin can. But he also found a small leather notebook. He handed the tin to Lady Li while he flipped through the notebook. The notebook contained the family names and given names of young women, including the ones that Hungjian had mentioned. There were also dates and amounts of money. It didn't say what the money was for, but any man would know. It was similar to the ledgers madams often kept for their flower houses.

Lady Li gasped when she saw how much money was in the tin. "This...this is a small fortune," she said. "Do prostitutes usually earn this much money?"

Inspector Gong looked at the money and back at the book. "There is a significant amount of money here not accounted for in the ledger."

"So where did it come from?" Lady Li asked.

"Maybe he was blackmailing some of the girls and was smart enough not to record it in his ledger," he said.

Lady Li shook her head and closed the tin, handing it back to Inspector Gong. "How did Hungjian know where the money was?" she asked. "Seems like something he wouldn't tell anyone about."

"Fanhua and Hungjian were lovers," he told her, taking the tin.

Lady Li froze, her eyes wide once again. Inspector Gong chuckled. "I guess I hadn't told you that yet."

She slapped his arm. "No. How long have you known?"

"I learned that Fanhua was a cut sleeve a few days ago," he said. "But I only found out about his relationship with Hungjian before I came here."

"But Fanhua was also having affairs with all the women in the ledger," Lady Li said. "And Hungjian, isn't he also very popular with the young female patrons?"

"Very," Inspector Gong said. "He was sleeping with some of the women as well. He said that he and Fanhua were saving for their future."

"What a mess," Lady Li said, pacing and shaking her head. "It is terrible what these young people have been through, have put themselves through, in order to survive. To find happiness. And now Fanhua is dead. And how does Wangshu figure into all this?"

"We should ask Wangshu," the inspector said. "She claimed to be having some sort of relationship with Fanhua as well. But I think she was lying about that."

"I think she lied about being attacked as well," Lady Li said. "She knows I want to help her. Why is she not being truthful with me?"

"Hopefully she will tell us," he said.

"We should head back to the house," Lady Li said. "If she is lying about her role in all this, who knows what she is capable of."

She tried to walk past him, toward the door, but he reached out and grabbed her wrist. "Wait," he said.

She looked back at her wrist, then up at him. He didn't need to say more before she flew into his arms and he held her tight as they kissed. He dropped the notebook and tin to the floor with a clatter, but neither of them cared. He opened his mouth, taking all of her into him. Her taste. Her scent. She reached up behind his neck, rocking forward on her pot-bottom shoes to meet his every move. His hands groped her breasts and then moved down her body, pulling her up to him.

He held her as he moved her back toward a small couch.

It wouldn't be comfortable, but it would do. He placed her down and laid on top of her, pulling her gown up to her hips. He kissed down her neck, and her back arched as she moaned. He moved his hand up her gown to touch her.

"No! Stop!" she cried grabbing his wrist.

"What?" he asked, looking up at her.

"We can't," she said, shaking her head and panting. "We...we can't."

He looked around, wondering if someone had caught them. "Why?" he asked when he didn't see anyone.

"Swan!" she said. "She's to be your wife."

He grunted and moved back to suckling on her neck. "Forget her," he said. "I love you. I want you. Right now, I *need* you."

She let out a whimpering cry and held him tight. For a moment, he thought everything was fine. That they would be able to once again make love as he had imagined. As he couldn't stop thinking about. But then she pushed him away again.

"I can't," she said scooting away and sitting up. She dropped her forehead to her head and sniffed back a cry. "I can't do it to her."

"But what about us?" he asked, grabbing her wrist. She looked up at him with wet eyes. "We need each other. We love each other."

"I guess Fanhua and Hungjian weren't the only people who wanted something they couldn't have," she said sadly.

He kissed the back of her fingertips. "Life is cruel, isn't it?" he asked.

She stood up and tugged at his hand for him to follow her. "Let's go talk to Wangshu and put this case to bed."

He gathered up the notebook and tin. "Go ahead without me," he said. "I'll walk."

She nodded and left the room first.

He knew that she would have arrived at the theater in her sedan chair. It would be improper for him to be seen riding back with her. Besides, the walk would help him cool down, even in this heat.

18

Lady Li berated herself during the ride back to her house. She was angry with herself for giving into Inspector Gong. Angry at herself for pushing him away. Angry at not being free to do what she wanted with her life. She could be completely content with every other aspect of her life if she could only have him. The one thing she wanted most in the world was the one thing she couldn't have.

She was a fool for torturing herself over him. She had to stop thinking about him. Stop fantasizing about him at night. Stop helping him with his cases. She had to let him go. After his marriage to Swan, she couldn't see him ever again.

When she arrived home, Dr. Xue was just leaving. She rudely crossed the courtyard so she wouldn't have to speak to him, but their eyes crossed paths anyway. He stared at her and pressed his lips in a thin frown. It was as though he knew what she had done. What she and Inspector Gong almost did in that dressing room. She tore her eyes away and went to her office where she could be alone for a few moments and collect herself before Inspector Gong arrived.

"Lady Li!" Wangshu exclaimed as Lady Li opened the door to her office.

"What are you doing in here?" Lady Li asked. Her eyes scanned the room quickly, trying to make sense of the scene before Wangshu tried to cover her tracks.

Wangshu was holding a brush in her hand and there was a paper with writing on it on the desk. Wangshu grabbed the paper and started to crumple it up.

"I was just leaving you a note, thanking you for your kind hospitality," Wangshu said. "But now you are here, so I can just tell you in person."

Lady Li stepped toward her with her hand outstretched. "Then let me see the note."

Wangshu crumpled paper behind her back. "Oh, it's nothing, really—"

"Give it to me," Lady Li ordered, her face hard. "Now."

Wangshu gulped and handed Lady Li the paper.

"'By the time you read this,'" Lady Li quoted. "'I will be long gone.' Well, we can't add fortune teller to your list of talents." Lady Li angrily crumpled up the paper and tossed it across the room. "You aren't going anywhere."

"Please, Lady Li," Wangshu begged. "It's too dangerous for me here. I don't want to lose my head!"

Lady Li sighed, feeling sorry for the girl. "I understand that you are scared. But running away only makes you look guilty. You are safe here. Just give the inspector more time."

"More time?" Wangshu asked. "How much more? How long do I have to live in this state of limbo?"

"Stop being so dramatic," Lady Li chided. "I think being under house arrest in a fine mansion with plenty of food and servants to wait on you for a few days is worth saving your life."

Wangshu gasped and crossed her arms. Lady Li suspected that Wangshu was far more pampered than she realized. Unlike most opera performers who lived at the whims of the people and often scrapped by for a living, Wangshu was patroned by the empress and normally lived in the palace. She never had to worry about where her next meal was going to come from or if she would have a job the next day.

"Mama! Mama!" Second Daughter yelled, skipping into the room. "Watch me! Watch me!"

"What is it, darling?" Lady Li asked, slipping onto a chair and forcing a smile to her mouth.

Second Daughter held out one hand and placed the other on her hip as she walked in a circle. Then she smiled and cocked her head. She opened her mouth and recited,

"Surrounded by green hills, lush from summer rains,

There is a lake that shimmers, and hides a precious secret.

Visitors from near and far, stroll the water's edge.

They all hope to catch a glimpse, of the woman from their dreams."

She couldn't quite sing the words. Opera was a very specific type of signing that took years of practice. But she spoke in a defined, rhythmic fashion as she moved her hands and held her head just so as she spoke the opening lines of *The Legend of the White Snake Lady*.

Lady Li clapped. "Looks like someone has been getting secret opera lessons."

"There hasn't been much else to do around here," Wangshu said. "And your daughter is an apt student."

"What did you think, Mama?" Second Daughter asked. "Can Wangshu keep teaching me?"

Lady Li leaned over and kissed her little girl on the head. The child was talented, there was no question about that. But was it right to get her hopes up? She should be tending to her lessons—learning to read and write and quote poetry—and improving her embroidery skills, all things that her future in-laws would be looking for in a wife for their son.

But as she looked down into the beaming face of her youngest child, her baby, she couldn't bear to stop her from doing something that brought her so much joy.

"Of course, darling," Lady Li said. "That is, if Wangshu is going to be around to teach you." She raised her eyebrow and looked pointedly at Wangshu.

Wangshu grunted. "That's a fine way to get me to stay," she mumbled.

"Yay!" Second Daughter said as she ran around the room a few times and then out the door, undoubtedly to brag to her elder sister.

"You know," Wangshu said, "it's past time for your girls to drop their milk names and choose names that reflect their personality."

"They are my only children," Lady Li said. "I hate any reminders that they are growing up. It's happening far too quickly."

"You can't stop the future from coming," Wangshu said. "All you can do is prepare for it."

"How did you get to be so wise?" Lady Li asked, playfully slapping Wangshu's arm.

Wangshu laughed. "No one ever accused me of being wise before."

"Well, running away right now would be quite stupid,"

Lady Li said. "You must stay. You must trust me. If for some reason the inspector doesn't find the real killer, you still needn't worry. I'll protect you."

Wangshu sighed, and they squeezed each other's hands. "So what do we do next?"

"The inspector is on his way here," Lady Li said. "Hopefully he will have an idea. But he will have some hard questions for you."

"Like what?" Wangshu asked, wringing her hands like she was a little nervous.

"Like why you've been lying about your relationship with Fanhua," the inspector said as he entered the room.

Lady Li stood up and walked to the door. "Where is Eunuch Bai?" she asked. "Why didn't he announce you?"

"He doesn't know I'm here," he said. "The good doctor let me in on his way out. He said Swan is resting. Maybe Eunuch Bai is tending to her."

Lady Li hmphed in annoyance. "You still shouldn't admit yourself," she mumbled.

Wangshu had turned away, standing there silently, perhaps hoping Inspector Gong would forget the question he had asked her. But she was out of luck.

"Well?" the inspector said, crossing his arms and waiting for an answer.

"What makes you think I was lying?" she asked. "We were friendly. I wouldn't kill him."

"You weren't that friendly," he said. "Fanhua resenting you for taking his place, for forcing him to act like a man. And if you weren't one of his paying admirers, he wouldn't have taken you for a lover."

"Paying admirers?" Wangshu asked. "What are you saying?"

"Fanhua was prostituting himself," Lady Li said. "He

preferred men but would show affection to the female patrons for a fee."

"That's terrible," Wangshu said, slipping into a nearby chair. "I had no idea..."

"No idea that Fanhua was a cut sleeve?" the inspector asked. "Or that he was charging his admirers for his affections?"

"None of it," Wangshu admitted. "He hated me from the moment I entered the theater. But I was afraid you would think I killed him if you knew that. I didn't really know anything about his life."

Inspector Gong walked over and handed the ledger to Wangshu. "Do you know any of these women?"

Wangshu opened the book and looked the pages over. "Is this...what he was charging...goodness me."

"Do you see something odd?" Lady Li asked.

"No," Wangshu said. "I just should have known. This type of lifestyle is common among actors. Many people would pay good money to live out a fantasy. I'm just surprised he was charging so little. He was so popular."

"I think he may have been blackmailing some of those girls to get more money out of them," the inspector said. "What do you think?"

"It's possible," she said, handing the book back. "But I don't know for certain. Those women hated me even more than Fanhua did."

"Hated you enough to frame you for Fanhua's murder?" the inspector asked.

Wangshu shook her head in disbelief. "But they loved him, didn't they? Why would they use me to kill him?"

"Maybe one of these girls hated him enough to want him dead," Lady Li said, "but loved him too much to do the job herself."

"It's just so crazy," Wangshu said.

"I've never known a murderer to be completely sane," the inspector said.

"So what do we do now?" Lady Li asked. "How do we find out which woman was the killer?"

"Changpu wants the next performance go on as planned," the inspector said. "He hired Hungjian to take the role of the wusheng. And he wants Wangshu to return to play the dan one more time."

Wangshu stood up and paced. "Oh no," she said, shaking her head and wringing her hands. "I...I can't go back there. That...that's the real reason I left. Every time I looked at that stage, I felt so sick. I can still feel...feel the way the sword went into Fanhua's stomach..." She collapsed back into her chair, her face blanched. Lady Li ran to her side, afraid she was going to faint. She could feel Wangshu trembling.

"Inspector," Lady Li said. "We can't make her go back."

"But the killer could return," he said. "When she finds out that Wangshu wasn't arrested for the crime, she could come back and finish the job."

"You want to use me as bait?" Wangshu asked. "What if the crazy girl kills *me*?"

"That's a risk I'm willing to take," the inspector said.

Wangshu let out a despondent wail. "How could you?" she cried. "Am I not a person? Don't I matter just as much as Fanhua?"

"Of course, you do," Lady Li said, patting Wangshu's hand and shooting a look at Inspector Gong. "I'm sure we can think of another plan."

"I suppose we could just say Wangshu is going to be there," he said. "And hope the killer makes her appearance."

"But if Wangshu isn't there, why would the killer come out of hiding?" Lady Li asked. "No, your plan to use someone as bait is a good one. But we can't use Wangshu."

"Well, who do you—" the inspector started to ask, but then he cut himself off when he saw the determined look on Lady Li's face. "No. No, you are not going to try to lure a murderer to kill you."

"Why not?" Lady Li asked. "If it was a good enough plan for Wangshu it's a good enough plan for me. And you'll be there to protect me, won't you?"

"But you don't look anything like me," Wangshu said. "And you can't sing."

"I won't really be singing. If the murderer appears, the farce won't need to continue. And if she doesn't appear, I'll just have Changpu announce that Wangshu took ill or something. As for what I look like, don't opera performers wear masks?" Lady Li asked. "I can wear a mask."

"Ugh," Wangshu groaned. "I thought you knew a thing or two about opera. I'm not a face-changer or eighty years old. I paint my face. Only older performers used masks."

"Still," Lady Li said. "I can just wear a mask to enter the enter the theater. It will be good enough to convince the crowd outside that Wangshu is there."

"But I don't have a mask," Wangshu said. "Most opera performers would have sold them or traded them away years ago."

"What about one of Hungjian's masks?" the inspector asked. "We could borrow one of those."

"They don't look anything like Peking opera faces," Wangshu explained. "And they are made of fabric, not wood. Anyone watching would immediately know something was going on. No, you'd have to wear a Peking opera mask, but I don't have any."

Lady Li smiled. "You said many of the masks have been sold. In that case, I think I know where I might find one."

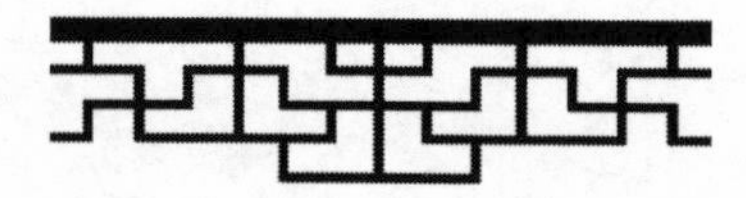

"This is surely one of the most beautiful homes I have seen here in the city," the American said in his distinct southern drawl as he walked through the courtyard.

"Mr. Big," Lady Li said as she walked over to him and shook his hand. "Thank you for coming."

"Well, of course, darlin'," he said. "I could not resist an invitation from the mysterious Lady Li. I had a suspicion that you were better than you let on when you tried to pass as a maid in the legation, but I had no idea you were this well off."

Lady Li smiled. She spoke fairly good English but still found some of Mr. Big's colloquialisms confusing. Inspector Gong stood nearby, but since he didn't speak English at all he stayed quiet.

"Did you bring the items I asked for?" Lady Li asked.

"Oh yes," he said opening his case. "You are lucky I had a few in stock. These normally sell like hotcakes to the foreign traders." He pulled out several masks, all painted in blue, green, and yellow, but they were all masculine characters.

"Oh dear," Lady Li said, looking them over. "Do you have any of female characters?"

"Those are quite rare," Mr. Big said. "Peking Opera simply doesn't have many female characters, which is a shame. Their faces and costumes are so exquisite. But you are in luck that I do happen to have one."

He pulled out a mask painted white with pink eyelids and long thin eyebrows. It was combined with an elaborate headdress designed like a blue peacock. It had most likely been designed for an empress or princess character.

"It's incredible," Lady Li said. "And exactly what I need."

"I am glad to hear it," Mr. Big said. "Anything you need, you just let me know. I am your humble servant."

Lady Li waved Eunuch Bai over. "Eunuch Bai is the head of my household," Lady Li explained. "He doesn't speak much English, but he handles my accounts. He will make sure you are paid."

Eunuch Bai started to give Mr. Big a bow, but Mr. Big reached out and took one of Eunuch's Bai's hands and shook it.

"Such an honor to meet you, sir," Mr. Big said while Lady Li translated. "I have never met a real eunuch before. I heard they only serve in the Forbidden City, a place I am certainly forbidden to ever enter." He laughed at his own joke even though it didn't exactly translate to Chinese.

"The empress was kind enough to allow me to take Eunuch Bai with me when I left the palace," Lady Li told Mr. Big.

"You actually know the empress?" Mr. Big asked, his mouth agape. Lady Li gave a small smile and nod. "Oh honey, you and I need a have a long chat at some point. My sisters would just die if they found out I know a real Chinese princess!"

"I'm not a princess—" Lady Li tried to say, but Mr. Big cut her off with a wave of his hand.

"The details don't really matter." He returned to Eunuch Bai. "And the stories I bet you could tell me. We must find a way to communicate..."

19

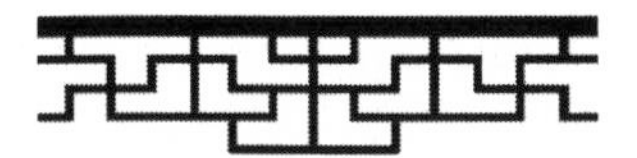

Lady Li ran her fingers over the sequins of her elaborate opera costume. She had never worn anything so heavy before, not even her wedding gown. Her headdress jingled as her chair-bearers carried her through town and toward the White Lotus Theater. She breathed slowly in and out to calm her nerves. Even though Inspector Gong and his men would be at the theater, she couldn't help but be nervous. She was planning on meeting a murderer tonight.

As they got closer to the theater, the sound of raised voices grew louder. When the chair-bearers stopped and placed the sedan chair on the ground, the voices exploded into a torrent of anger.

"Kill the whore!" a man yelled.

"Justice for Fanhua!" a woman cried.

The chair rocked as though someone had pushed it, and Lady Li yelped. What was happening out there? She was about to tell her men to take her back home when someone opened the door flap.

Inspector Gong stuck his head inside. "We better get

inside before things get out of control," he said, holding his hand out to her.

"*Before* they get out of control?" she asked, but she took a gulp and grabbed his hand.

He helped pull her from her seat and out onto the street. She was shocked to see dozens of people outside yelling and shaking their fists at her. Inspector Gong wrapped his arm around her and helped usher her toward the door where one of his men was standing guard.

Someone threw something that hit Lady Li in the back of the head. She ducked as she cried out. She glanced down at her feet and saw an apple rolling across the ground. Several people laughed at her while others continued with their angry jeers.

It was a good thing Wangshu did not return to the theater. It was terrifying. The people were either angry at her for performing on stage or for killing Fanhua. The fact that what she was doing was completely legal or that she had not been charged for Fanhua's death didn't matter to these people. They were simply out for blood.

When they were finally inside the theater, Lady Li was surprised she didn't feel more relief. Theater-goers who had purchased tickets were already inside, and they immediately started staring at her and murmuring.

"I need to go back outside and help get the crowd under control," Inspector Gong said.

Lady Li gripped his arm. "Wait," she said, her voice muffled behind the mask. "You can't leave me. What about the...you know..."

"Don't worry," he said. "I'll be back soon. Some of my men are here inside the theater as well. As is Prince Kung." He looked up at the balcony and waved. Her eyes followed and she saw the prince sitting next to his wife waving back at her. She raised her hand back at him. Did he know she was Lady Li? Or did he think she was really Wangshu? For some reason, having the prince there almost made her more nervous.

"You'll be safe in your dressing room," the inspector said before she could ask what the prince knew. "I'll join you there soon." With that, he quickly slipped back outside.

Lady Li turned back around. Her stomach a bundle of nerves. She couldn't move.

Then, she heard clapping from the balcony. She looked up and saw that the prince—along with his wife and the rest of the guests in his box—was clapping for her. The rest of the theater-goers followed suit, clapping and smiling at her.

She wasn't sure why. Just to be encouraging? Proud that she had dared to return for a second performance? She had no idea, and she didn't have time to think about it. The play would be starting soon. She gave everyone a small bow and then walked down the aisle toward her dressing room.

Once in the dressing room, she closed the door and paced. Wangshu's character of Xueyan did not appear for the first few scenes, so the patrons would get to see at least some of the opera before Lady Li would have to feint illness and Changpu would have to cancel the rest of the show. *If* he canceled it. It was not unheard of for actors to simply work around surprises to their show in order to keep a performance going.

The plan was for Lady Li to stay in the dressing room, and whoever tried to break in must be the killer. Inspector Gong would then rush over and grab whoever it was and get a confession out of her. Or possibly him. They still didn't really know who they were looking for, or if the villain would even appear, but they didn't have a better plan at this point.

Lady Li closed the door, but she wasn't able to lock it because she didn't have a key. Her heart beat fast in her chest. She willed herself to calm down as she searched the room for some way to bolt the door. As she rifled through a crate of props, she heard the door squeak open behind her.

"Baoah?" Lady Li said as she turned and faced the girl who entered the room.

"Wangshu," Baoah replied, stepping into the room.

Lady Li realized that Baoah did not recognize her voice from behind the mask. Was Baoah the killer? She never would have imagined...But her name had been in the ledger they found. It was possible...

"I'm surprised you returned after what happened," Baoah said.

Changpu's powerful voice rang out and drifted into the room as the show began.

"The theater is my life," Lady Li said in her best imitation of Wangshu's voice.

"It's *my* life," Baoah growled. "It was Fanhua's life. You ruined everything!"

"I...I don't know what you mean..." Lady Li said, growing worried. Where was Inspector Gong?

"Fanhua loved me," Baoah said.

"But...you were paying for that love," Lady Li foolishly said. She should have just let Baoah say and think whatever she wanted.

"Everyone has to earn a living," Baoah said. "And one day he would earn enough to run away from this place."

But not with you, Lady Li thought to herself. So Fanhua had let Baoah think that he was saving money to leave the theater for her, not Hungjian. But what went wrong?

"Then why kill him?" Lady Li asked.

"Because you ruined his life," Baoah said. "He couldn't live with himself playing a man. He hated what he saw when he looked in the mirror. Didn't you see how despondent he was? How miserable? That's why he played the general so badly. He hated the role. He hated himself. I saw his face, the tears, when he looked at himself in the mirror during rehearsal."

"I'm sorry," Lady Li said. So Baoah had also been backstage on the day of the murder. That must have been when she switched the sword. "I was only doing what I was ordered to do—"

"Liar!" Baoah said, stepping closer.

Lady Li shrunk back. She looked around, trying to find a way past Baoah and into the hallway, but in the small room her options were limited.

"You love performing," Baoah said. "Being on the stage. Parading yourself like a whore. You didn't give a damn about Fanhua!"

Lady Li didn't reply. There was no point in trying to correct Baoah's beliefs. She had concocted a story in her head and there was no changing it.

"He had to get out of here," Baoah continued. "He had to leave the theater. But he needed money."

"So that's why he started blackmailing you," Lady Li said. "Instead of planning to leave in the distant future, he wanted to escape now, so he blackmailed you for money."

"You figured it out," Baoah said. "How?"

"I found his ledger," Lady Li said. "He kept a record of all the women he was sleeping with and the money they were paying him."

"What?" Baoah screeched. "Where is it? Give it to me!"

"I can't," Lady Li said. "That inspector has it."

Baoah gasped. "I'll be ruined!" she cried. "How could you do this to me?"

"Me?" Lady Li asked. "You did this to yourself! You gave away your virtue, your reputation. This is all on you."

"What do you know about it?" Baoah cried, tears streaming down her face. "You're just some worthless opera singer. No one cares about locking you away your whole life. Keeping you in a box like a precious pearl. You have no idea what it is like to live your life in a prison."

Lady Li knew exactly what life as a young aristocrat was like, but she couldn't admit to that, not when she was supposed to be playing Wangshu.

"But why involve me in this?" Lady Li asked. "If Fanhua was blackmailing you, why not just kill him?"

"Because if you had never come here, never stole the role of the dan, none of this would have happened," Baoah said. "Women shouldn't be on the stage. It's an abomination. If you killed Fanhua, your head would roll and women would never be able to act on stage again."

"So you were trying to meet both ends," Lady Li said. "You wanted to both kill Fanhua and frame Wan...me. Quite clever. You almost got away with it."

"Almost," Baoah said. "But that stupid investigator never arrested you. Why? Did you sleep with him?"

"I'm not like you," Lady Li said.

"It doesn't matter," Baoah said, pulling a short sword out of her sleeve. "No one will be surprised to find you dead."

"Baoah," Lady Li gasped. "Stop! Don't do this!"

Baoah lunged toward Lady Li, who screamed but realized that the audience must not be able to hear her over the orchestra and Changpu's booming voice.

Lady Li grabbed a clothing rack and pulled it in front of her. Baoah fell into the clothes, getting tangled up in them.

Lady Li pushed the clothes and Baoah away from her, creating a small gap she could escape through, but she had forgotten how heavy the costume was. She wasn't able to move very quickly, and by the time she reached the door, Baoah was right behind her.

Lady Li flung the door open just as Baoah lunged at her again. The two of them stumbled into the hallway. Lady Li grabbed Baoah's wrists and did her best to hold her back, but she lost her balance on her pot-bottom shoes and felt herself fall backward. They both crashed into—and then through—the wall of the hallway and onto the stage.

Changpu yelped as he jumped out the way. The audience let out a collective gasp. The three other actors playing demons from hell all jumped around like crazed monkeys.

Lady Li stood up, a little dazed, and straightened her mask and headdress. The audience laughed.

Baoah stood up and raised her sword. Her eyes bored into Lady Li.

"Stop this," Lady Li hissed. "It's over, you stupid girl!"

Baoah yelled and charged at Lady Li. With more room to move, Lady Li was no longer so intimidated by Baoah. Lady Li grabbed a lance one of the other actors had been carrying and used it to guard herself from Baoah's attack. The audience cheered as the two fought.

Baoah then used all her strength, bringing the sword down as hard as she could, breaking Lady Li's lance in two. Lady Li stepped back, unsure of what to do. But then someone tapped Baoah on the shoulder. Baoah looked behind her and saw Inspector Gong. The inspector backhanded her hard across the face, sending her to the ground.

Lady Li was so relieved to see the inspector, she ran across the stage into his arms. The audience clapped. The inspector lifted Lady Li's mask but held her face in his hands so no one could see who it really was as he kissed her.

The audience cheered once again as Changpu burst out into a love ballad. Inspector Gong's men dragged Baoah off the stage. Lady Li and Inspector Gong left the stage through the hole she had created when she fell through the wall.

"We shouldn't have done that," Lady Li said once they were backstage.

"They will think it was Wangshu," Inspector Gong said. "It will make a good story for the newspapers tomorrow."

"Wait!" Lady Li called out as she saw the inspector's men taking Baoah away through a back door.

Baoah still seemed a bit stunned from the blow to her face. She had to blink a few times before she realized who was speaking to her.

"Lady...Li?" she asked. "What are you doing here? What is happening?"

"I was only pretending to be Wangshu as we tried to draw out the killer," Lady Li said. "And you fell right into our trap."

"No!" Baoah said. "I...Fanhua...Wangshu..." She flailed as she tried to come up with an excuse. If she revealed that Fanhua had been blackmailing her, her reputation would still be ruined. And everyone in the theater had seen her try to kill "Wangshu." There was no way for her to save herself.

"Take her to the Ministry of Justice," Inspector Gong ordered.

"I can't help but feel somewhat sorry for her," Lady Li said. "Fanhua only used her for her money, even before he started blackmailing her."

"Actions have consequences," the inspector said. "If we try to protect her, Wangshu will pay the price. Someone will have to answer for Fanhua's death."

Lady Li sighed. Had she acted any better? The only difference between Baoah's affair with Fanhua and Lady Li's affair with Inspector Gong was that Fanhua kept a record. If anyone learned of Lady Li's indiscretions, she would have to face the consequences as well.

Inspector Gong wrapped his arm around Lady Li's shoulders, but she moved away from him.

"I should go home," she said. "Tell Wangshu what happened. She will be anxious to know I am safe."

"Of course," he said, though clearly a bit disappointed.

"Tomorrow," she continued, "let us know what will happen to Baoah."

He nodded. "Tomorrow, then."

20

Inspector Gong slept soundly for the first time in weeks, and he didn't feel the need to get up early and rush out of the house. He awoke to the normal sounds of people in his house starting their day and the smell of the servants making breakfast. He looked over and ran his hand over the side of the bed where his wife should be sleeping...whoever she was.

He knew it would be Swan.

No matter how much he wished it could be Lady Li he woke up to, he knew it could never happen.

He could hear his mother barking orders to one of his sisters-in-law and chuckled. As if Lady Li would ever allow a woman—even a mother-in-law—to speak to her like that. For the very fact that Lady Li didn't have to answer to any other woman was enough for her to never leave her situation. Here, not only would she have to answer to his mother, but his brothers' wives and even his sisters, until they married out. Lady Li would be at the bottom of the hierarchy in this family. She could never live her life like that.

Swan, on the other hand, would adjust. She was used to

having no rank, no real place in the family. She would thrive in a large family with lots of children and a never-ending list of things to do. And eventually, she would have her own children to care for...he hoped.

Yes, a wife and children. It was time.

He sat up and was looking for his slippers when he suddenly heard his sister Daiyu crying. He couldn't make out what she was saying, but his mother was berating her instead of comforting her.

Then he remembered that Daiyu was one of the young women who would sneak out to see Fanhua's performances. A knot formed in his belly as he pulled out Fanhua's journal and furiously scanned the pages looking for her name. He hadn't seen it when he looked through the journal before, but he hadn't considered that he might find it.

He breathed a sigh of relief when he didn't see her name.

After a moment, he couldn't hear Daiyu anymore, but there was a small tapping on his door.

"Enter," he said, expecting a maid, but was surprised to see his mother poke her head in. "Oh, sorry, Ma," he said, standing up and offering her a chair.

"Your room is a disaster," she said. "I think I raised a pig."

He smirked and then took a seat back on the bed. "What's wrong with Daiyu?"

His mother grimaced. "That opera singer, the man who dressed like a woman, he is dead. Murdered."

He nodded. "She knew about that a few days ago."

"Her friend, the Liu girl, was arrested for the crime!" his mother said, concern etched across her brow.

"I had no idea she knew Baoah," he said. "But I should

have assumed it was possible when I found out that Daiyu enjoyed the opera. I will apologize to her."

"She doesn't need an apology," his mother said. "She needs a husband. This family has grown too big for me to manage. Biyu told me that Daiyu has been sneaking out to see the opera performances."

Inspector Gong didn't say anything, but that told his mother all she needed to know.

"You knew," she said, shaking her head in disappointment.

"I didn't want to worry you—" he started to say, but she raised her hand, cutting him off.

"It doesn't matter now," she said. "But we are lucky her reputation is safe. This could have gone very badly for her, for all of us."

He nodded. He should have considered his own sister in all of this...

"It is time she was married," his mother continued. "But I need to know your plan first. If you marry Lady Swan, it could...*alter* Daiyu's marriage prospects."

"In a good or bad way?" Inspector Gong asked.

"I don't know," his mother said, wringing her hands. "I don't know anyone with a Manchu girl in their family. Some people might only see her as an idle curiosity; others might view mingling with the invaders as a great betrayal to our inheritance."

"But most people know our family to be Qing loyalists," Inspector Gong said. "Baba has worked in the Ministry of Letters for decades. Yeye even—"

"I know," his mother said, interrupting. "But this *is* different. You can't deny it. Working with the Manchu for money or position is not the same as taking their women to bed. To giving the Manchu more sons."

He stood and paced. While he knew that some people outside the family might be offended by his marriage to Swan, he never considered it could cost Daiyu a good match.

"Would it be better if I don't wed?" he asked. "Because my position on this has not changed. If I cannot marry Swan, I don't wish to marry."

"An unmarried son is an insult to me and your father," his mother said. "But it is not an insult to the Han people. Remaining as you are will not change things for Daiyu."

"Is that what you want?" he asked. "You would rather I remain single for Daiyu's sake?"

His mother held her breath as she stared at her son. What did he think would happen? That he would change his mind and agree to marry a Han girl to keep her from passing out?

Finally, she blew out her cheeks. "No," she grumbled. "It doesn't matter. A daughter is like water on the floor."

He was all too familiar with the common belief that investing in daughters—money, education, even affection—was often viewed as a waste since after they were married out, they rarely returned to the home of the birth. But he could see tears pool on the edge of his mother's eyes and knew that she didn't really believe this. In fact, Daiyu and Biyu both should already be married. His mother had been delaying in order to keep them with her for as long as possible. They were her last daughters, her last pearls.

"I could wait to marry Swan until after Daiyu's marriage, if that would help," he offered.

His mother stood up, shaking her head. "No. I just needed to know how set you were on the marriage. If there was any chance of preventing it."

"I am sorry to have failed your final test," he said with a half-cocked smile.

"My children will be the death of me," she said, pointing an accusatory finger at him. "As yours will be of you. You will understand. You'll see!"

"I'll tell Lady Li to expect your visit to finalize arrangements," he said as she left the room.

But after the humor of torturing his mother wore off, he realized he would need to speak to Lady Li about his marriage to Swan one more time. When they had been alone together in the dressing room, she wanted him. He could feel it in the touch of her hand, the taste of her kiss, in the breaths from her lips. She pushed him away, yes, but only so she wouldn't insult Swan because she thought he was still going to marry her. Lady Li had called Swan his betrothed. She thought the marriage was a foregone conclusion. But there was still a chance to call it off. His mother had hoped he would choose bachelorhood over marriage. She would still let him walk away.

He had to give Lady Li one more chance to call off his marriage to Swan.

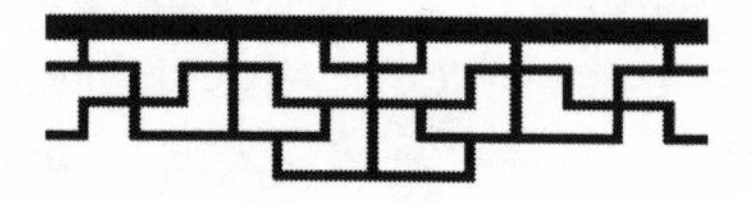

As Inspector Gong crossed Lady Li's garden, he saw Lady Li, Wangshu, and Swan all sitting together, chatting and laughing over a pot of tea. At first, he thought he might be intruding, but they all smiled when they saw him.

"Ladies," he said, offering them an exaggerated bow.

"Inspector Gong," they all said in unison as they rose and gave him a bow in return. Well, Wangshu and Swan bowed; Lady Li only nodded her head.

"Have a seat," Lady Li said, motioning toward a pillow next to Wangshu.

"You all seem to be having an enjoyable morning," he said as Swan served him tea. He tried to meet her eyes, but she kept them downcast, as was proper.

"I feel like I can breathe for the first time in days," Wangshu said. "I can't wait to go home."

"You mean back to the palace?" Inspector Gong asked. "You won't be returning to the theater?"

"Never!" Wangshu said. "I have had enough of the opera scene outside the safety of the walls of the Forbidden City."

"But what about paving the way for future female opera singers?" he asked. "Isn't that what this whole exercise was about? What the empress wanted?"

"I'm not sure the world is ready for female opera singers," Wangshu said.

Just then, Lady Li's daughters ran across the garden, yelling and swinging wooden swords. Second Daughter, though, was much more calculated in her movements, swinging her sword over her head, leaping through the air. First Daughter rushed over and pushed her sister to the ground playfully and then stood over her in triumph. The adults all laughed.

"Though, maybe I can still focus on training the next generation of female opera performers," Wangshu said. "Who knows what the future will hold."

"You will have to come back and keep giving Second

Daughter lessons," Lady Li said. "She would be devastated if you stopped."

"I will," Wangshu said.

"What will happen to the young woman you arrested?" Swan asked, and a morose feeling settled over all of them.

"I remanded her to the Ministry of Justice last night," the inspector said. "The chief minister said a conviction and sentence would be swift in coming."

No one said anything after that. They all knew that the only outcome for Baoah would be death.

Wangshu stood up. "I am going to go finish packing," she said. "I am sure my mother is anxious to see me again."

They all said their goodbyes and silence fell over them for a moment.

"I spoke to Dr. Xue on his way out yesterday," Inspector Gong said to Swan. "He said you had made much improvement."

She smiled and dared to look up at him for a quick second before returning her eyes to her teacup. "Yes," she said. "I am feeling much better. I am not fully healed yet. I am very tired and sometimes...I still have cravings. But I am sure I will be well in time."

"I am glad to hear it," he said.

She nearly dropped her cup on the table as she fell to her knees before him.

"I promise I will be a good wife to you," she blurted out in tears. "I will honor and submit to you and to your honorable mother. I will make sure you never regret marrying me. I will...I will give you sons!"

"Swan!" Lady Li snapped.

"O...kay," he said, gripping her thin forearms in his hands and pulling her to her feet. "Please, calm yourself. I am sure you will be an excellent wife."

"Forgive me," she said, wiping her eyes with her sleeve. "I just never thought I would get another chance..."

"I understand," he said as he released her arms, hoping she had the strength to hold herself up.

"Swan," Lady Li said firmly. "You should return to your room and wash your face."

"Of course," Swan said. She bowed to them both as she walked away backward, as though she was leaving the presence of the emperor.

"I'm sorry about that," Lady Li said. "She has made progress under Dr. Xue's care, but she has been very emotional lately. I'm not sure—"

"There is no need to apologize," Inspector Gong said. "She is both excited and possibly scared. She has met my mother, after all."

Lady Li chuckled. "Speaking of your mother, I am surprised she has not requested another meeting. We haven't finalized arrangements."

"I think she was waiting on me," he said. "I have been so busy with this case, we hadn't spoken in days."

"Waiting on you?" Lady Li asked. "But you had already consented. Why would she need to speak with you again except to inform you about the wedding date?"

"She...wanted to give me another chance to turn the match down," he said.

"Oh..." Lady Li said softly. "And what did you say?"

The fact that she thought he might have changed his mind about marrying told him that at least a very small part of her hoped he did. Why? Did she think they had any chance of a future together? Perhaps not as husband and wife, but as lovers?

"I told her I would let her know this afternoon," he lied.

"I...I wanted to check in with you one last time. I will not marry Swan if you tell me not to."

"Why must I make the decision?" Lady Li said. "Why is it on my shoulders what you do with your life?"

"You know why," he said. "I love you, and I would do whatever you tell me to. I would live as a beggar outside your door if you ordered it of me."

"You are a fool," Lady Li scoffed.

"Have you ever known a man to be otherwise?" he asked with a grin.

She shook her head and did her best not to smile back. They stood side by side and looked out over the garden and the children playing.

"I shall miss this," she finally said.

"Miss what?" he asked.

"The easy comfort we have," she said. "Your visits to my home. The way you look at me when you think I can't see you from the corner of my eye."

He blushed, not even realizing he had been staring at her.

"Just because I am marrying Swan doesn't mean that I won't ever see you again," he said.

"I know," she said. "But everything will change."

He wasn't sure how to respond to that. He knew she was right, but he was certain that his life would change in ways he hadn't even considered yet.

"My mother will call on you soon to finish the marriage arrangements," he said.

"I will be here waiting," she said.

He gave her a bow and then crossed the garden and walked out the gate.

Lady Li and Inspector Gong will return. Subscribe to my mailing list so you will be the first to find out when it is released!

http://www.twoamericansinchina.com/subscribe

ABOUT THE PUBLISHER

VISIT OUR WEBSITE
TO SEE ALL OF OUR HIGH QUALITY BOOKS:

http://www.redempresspublishing.com

Quality trade paperbacks, downloads, audio books, and books in foreign languages in genres such as historical, romance, mystery, and fantasy.

ABOUT THE AUTHOR

Amanda Roberts is a writer and editor who has been living in China since 2010. Amanda has an MA in English from the University of Central Missouri. She has been published in magazines, newspapers, and anthologies around the world and she regularly contributes to numerous blogs.

Website: http://www.twoamericansinchina.com
Newsletter:
http://www.twoamericansinchina.com/subscribe
Facebook:https://www.facebook.com/TwoAmericansinChina/
Twitter: https://twitter.com/2americanschina
InstaGram: https://www.instagram.com/shreddedpotatoart/
Pintrest: https://www.pinterest.com/amandachina/crazy-dumplings/
Goodreads: https://www.goodreads.com/Amanda_Roberts
Amazon: http://amzn.to/2s9QzAG
BookBub: https://www.bookbub.com/authors/amanda-roberts-2bfe99dd-ea16-4614-a696-84116326dcd1
Email: twoamericansinchina@gmail.com

Made in the USA
San Bernardino, CA
31 October 2018